THE LIGHTNING WITHIN

THE LIGHTNING WITHIN

An Anthology of Contemporary

American Indian Fiction

Edited and with an introduction by Alan R. Velie

University of Nebraska Press

Lincoln and London

To my father, & to the memory of my mother

Contents

American Indians have been composing narratives for thousands of years. Although a few works, like the Lenape epic *Walam Olum,* were preserved in pictographs, most of the rest were passed on orally. The earliest example of Indian writing in America dates back over two centuries to the biographical memoir Samson Occom completed in 1768. Although Indians published autobiographies, novels, short stories, and poems throughout the nineteenth and much of the twentieth century, their works were generally ignored by the American reading public. Occasionally writers like Charles Eastman and Alexander Posey achieved a brief notoriety, but to most Americans "Indian literature" would have seemed an oxymoron.

By the late 1960s the civil rights movement had brought to the American consciousness a heightened awareness of the richness of minority cultures. When Scott Momaday won the Pulitzer Prize for *House Made of Dawn* in 1969, he began a renaissance in Indian writing. It was not only that the time was right for ethnic writers; more important, Momaday's novel was an extremely powerful and poetic work. Momaday's ability to tell a story, and his masterful use of language, demonstrated that Indian writing was no longer of interest merely to anthropologists or others curious about Indian culture, but that it was to be taken seriously as literature.

Encouraged by Momaday's success and publishers' newfound interest in Indian works, a number of highly talented writers of fiction emerged, foremost among them the other authors included in this collection: James Welch, Leslie Silko, Gerald Vizenor, Simon Ortiz, Louise Erdrich, and Michael Dorris. These writers have gained some critical attention—academics have written about them in scholarly journals, and their works are usually reviewed in the *New York Times Book Review*—but by and large they are still not well known to most readers. It is the purpose of this book to address that problem by providing a selection of some of the best pieces of contemporary Indian fiction to serve as an introduction to the principal Indian novelists and short-story writers of the past twenty years.

Readers who enjoy the authors included here will want to seek out other works by them. I hope, too, that these readers will also move on to other sorts of Indian writing—the drama of Hanay Geigomah, the political and philosophical writings of Vine Deloria, and the poetry of Rayna Green, Diane Burns, and Paula Gunn Allen, to name just a few examples.

Indians are producing some of the best writing in America today. Reading it is a rich experience that tells us not only much about them, but much about ourselves as well.

N. Scott Momaday is the dean of American Indian writers. His works include two novels, *House Made of Dawn* (1968), from which our excerpt is taken, and *The Ancient Child* (1989). He has published *Angle of Geese* (1974) and *The Gourd Dancer* (1976), both collections of poems, and two memoirs, *The Way to Rainy Mountain* (1969) and *The Names* (1976). He is also a talented artist whose paintings and drawings have been exhibited widely throughout the Southwest.

Momaday's versatility may seem extraordinary to readers familiar with mainstream English and American writers, who normally limit themselves to one genre. Surprisingly, however, with the sole exception of Michael Dorris, every writer in this collection published a substantial amount of poetry before he or she published any fiction.

Momaday's paternal ancestors were Kiowa; on his mother's side there was one Cherokee forebear. He was born in the Kiowa and Comanche Indian Hospital in Lawton, Oklahoma, in 1934, and lived for several years in Mountain View, near Rainy Mountain in southwest Oklahoma, Kiowa country.

In 1936 Momaday's parents left Oklahoma for the Southwest. He grew up on Navajo and Jemez reservations in Arizona and New Mexico, attended the Universities of New Mexico and Virginia, and graduated from New Mexico in 1958. After a brief stint as a teacher in the Indian school in Bernalillo, New Mexico, Momaday went to Stanford on a one-year creative-writing scholarship. There he came under the influence of the poet and critic Yvor Winters, who adopted Momaday as a protégé; Scott stayed to earn a Ph.D. in American literature.

Since graduating from Stanford, Momaday has taught American and Native American literature at the Universities of California at Santa Barbara and Berkeley, at Stanford, and at Arizona, where he is currently a Regents Professor of English.

Having spent a great deal of time in both the Indian and white worlds, Momaday is naturally concerned with questions of ethnic identity. Although he was raised among Indians, they were not of his tribe, and to some extent he felt like an outsider among them. Consequently, the nature of identity, particularly what it means to be an Indian, is an important and complex theme in his work. To Momaday, Indian identity is an existential choice, "an act of imagination," as he says in *The Names*. This is true not only for individuals, but for tribes as well. The chapter anthologized here, "Tosamah's Story," describes the Kiowas as they redefined themselves as a people, changing their religion, means of subsistence—their whole outlook on life. Written at the beginning of Momaday's career, the selection reveals his concern with identity and other themes to which he has repeatedly returned: the mystery of the word, the metamorphosis of the bear, the nature of myth.

The sacredness of the word and the primacy of language to the Kiowas is a recurring theme in Momaday's writing. He says in "Man Made of Words," "We don't really begin to exist . . . until we convert ourselves into language." In "Tosamah's Story," John Big Bluff Tosamah, the self-ordained "Priest of the Sun," cites the Gospel according to John, which opens, "In the beginning was the Word." Tosamah's religion combines Indian ritual, the peyote ceremony, with Christian theology.

Although he is a villain in the novel, Tosamah is in many ways a reflection of Momaday. There is a physical resemblance: both are "big, lithe as a cat, narrow-eyed." And not only are both Kiowas, but when Tosamah tells his life story (the passage that begins "A single knoll . . ."), it is Momaday's life he is recounting, in the version Momaday published in *The Way to Rainy Mountain*.

The story that Tosamah briefly recounts of the boy who changes into a bear is a legend that Momaday embellished into a complete novel, *The Ancient Child*. Momaday's work is saturated in myth, and one must understand his ideas about myth to understand his fiction fully. To Momaday, myth and legend are the ways people make sense of the world. When Tosamah speaks of Devil's Tower (the rock pillar in Wyoming that Momaday was named after, in tribal fashion, as *Tsoai Talee,* "Rock Tree Boy"), he says that man "must never fail to explain such a thing to himself, or else he is estranged forever from the universe. Two centuries ago, because they could not do otherwise, the Kiowas made a legend at the base of the rock." That legend was the story of the boy who became a bear.

The Tai-me bundle was the sacred Sun Dance fetish of the Kiowas, the most powerful medicine, or sacred object, the tribe had.

There is a small silversided fish that is found along the coast of southern California. In the spring and summer it spawns on the beach during the first three hours after each of the three high tides following the highest tide. These fishes come by the hundreds from the sea. They hurl themselves upon the land and writhe in the light of the moon, the moon, the moon; they writhe in the light of the moon. They are among the most helpless creatures on the face of the earth. Fishermen, lovers, passers-by catch them up in their bare hands.

The Priest of the Sun lived with his disciple Cruz on the first floor of a two-story red-brick building in Los Angeles. The upstairs was maintained as a storage facility by the A. A. Kaul Office Supply Company. The basement was a kind of church. There was a signboard on the wall above the basement steps, encased in glass. In neat, movable white block letters on a black field it read:

LOS ANGELES
HOLINESS PAN-INDIAN RESCUE MISSION
Rev. J. B. B. Tosamah, Pastor & Priest of the Sun
Saturday 8:30 P.M.
"The Gospel According to John"
Sunday 8:30 P.M.
"The Way to Rainy Mountain"
Be kind to a white man today

The basement was cold and dreary, dimly illuminated by two 40-watt bulbs which were screwed into the side walls above the dais. This platform was made out of rough planks of various woods and dimensions, thrown together without so much as a hammer and nails; it stood seven or eight inches above the floor, and it supported the tin firebox and the crescent altar. Off to one side was a kind of lectern, decorated with red and yellow symbols of the sun and moon. In back of the dais there was a screen of purple drapery, threadbare and badly faded. On either side of the aisle which led to the altar there were chairs and crates, fashioned into pews. The walls were bare and gray and streaked with water. The only windows were small, rectangular openings near the ceiling, at ground level; the panes were covered over with a thick film of coal oil and dust, and spider webs clung to the frames or floated out like smoke across the room. The air was heavy and stale; odors of old smoke and incense lingered all around. The people had filed into the pews and were waiting silently.

Cruz, a squat, oily man with blue-black hair that stood out like spines from his head, stepped forward on the platform and raised his hands as if to ask for the quiet that already was. Everyone watched him for a moment; in the dull light his skin shone yellow with sweat. Turning slightly and extending his arm behind him, he said, "The Right Reverend John Big Bluff Tosamah."

There was a ripple in the dark screen; the drapes parted and the Priest of the Sun appeared, moving shadow-like to the lectern. He was shaggy and awful-looking in the thin, naked light: big, lithe as a cat, narrow-eyed, suggesting in the whole of his look and manner both arrogance and agony. He wore black like a cleric; he had the voice of a great dog:

"'*In principio erat Verbum.*' Think of Genesis. Think of how it was before the world was made. There was nothing, the Bible says, 'And the earth was without form, and void; and darkness was upon the face of the deep.' It was dark, and there was nothing. There were no mountains, no trees, no rocks, no rivers. There was nothing. But there was darkness all around, and in the darkness something happened. *Something happened!* There was a single sound. Far away in the darkness there was a single sound. Nothing made it, but it was there, and there was no one to hear it, but it was there. It was there, and there was nothing else. It rose up in the darkness, little and still, almost nothing in itself—like a single soft breath, like the wind arising; yes, like the whisper of the wind rising slowly and going out into the early morning. But there was no wind. There was only the sound, little and soft. It was almost nothing in itself, the smallest seed of sound—but it took hold of the darkness and there was light; it took hold of the stillness and there was motion forever; it took hold of the silence and there was sound. It was almost nothing in itself, a single sound, a word—a word broken off at the darkest center of the night and let go in the awful void, forever and forever. And it was almost nothing in itself. It scarcely was; but it *was,* and everything began."

Just then a remarkable thing happened. The Priest of the Sun seemed stricken; he let go of his audience and withdrew into himself, into some strange potential of himself. His voice, which had been low and resonant, suddenly became harsh and flat; his shoulders sagged and his stomach protruded, as if he had held his breath to the limit of endurance; for a moment there was a look of amazement, then utter carelessness in his face. Conviction, caricature, callousness: the remainder of his sermon was a going back and forth among these.

"Thank you *so* much, Brother Cruz. Good evening, blood brothers and sisters, and welcome, welcome. Gracious me, I see lots of new faces out there tonight. *Gracious me!* May the Great Spirit—can we knock off that talking in the back there?—be with you always.

" 'In the beginning was the Word.' I have taken as my text this evening the almighty Word itself. Now get this: 'There was a man sent from God, whose name was John. The same came for a witness, to bear witness of the Light, that all men through him might believe.' Amen, brothers and sisters, *Amen.* And the riddle of the Word, 'In the beginning was the Word. . . .' Now what do you suppose old John *meant* by that? That cat was a preacher, and, well, you know how it is with preachers; he had something big on his mind. Oh my, it was big; it was the *Truth,* and it was heavy, and old John hurried to set it down. And in his hurry he said too much. 'In the beginning was the Word, and the Word was with God, and the Word was God.' It was the Truth, all right, but it was more than the Truth. The Truth was overgrown with fat, and the fat was God. The fat was *John's* God, and God stood between John and the Truth. Old John, see, he got up one morning and caught sight of the Truth. It must have been like a bolt of lightning, and the sight of it made him blind. And for a moment the vision burned on in back of his eyes, and he *knew* what it was. In that instant he saw something he had never seen before and would never see again. That was the instant of revelation, inspiration, Truth. And old John, he must have fallen down on his knees. Man, he must have been shaking and laughing and crying and yelling and praying— all at the same time—and he must have been drunk and delirious with the Truth. You see, he had lived all his life waiting for that one moment, and it came, and it took him by surprise, and it was gone. And he said, 'In the beginning was the Word. . . .' And, man, right then and there he should have stopped. There was nothing more to say, but he went on. He had said all there was to say, everything, but he went on. 'In the beginning was the Word. . . .' Brothers and sisters, *that* was the Truth, the whole of it, the essential and eternal Truth, the bone and blood and muscle of the Truth. But he went on, old John, because he was a preacher. The perfect vision faded from his mind, and he went on. The instant passed, and then he had nothing but a memory. He was desperate and confused, and in his confusion he stumbled and went on. 'In the beginning was the Word, and the Word was with God, and the Word was God.' He went on to talk about Jews and Jerusalem, Levites and Pharisees, Moses and Philip and Andrew and Peter. Don't you see? Old John *had* to go on. That cat had a whole lot at stake. He couldn't let the Truth alone. He couldn't see that he had come to the end of the Truth, and he went on. He tried to make it bigger and better than it was, but instead he only demeaned and encumbered it. He made it soft and big with fat. He was a preacher, and he made a complex sentence of the Truth, two sentences, three, a paragraph. He made a sermon and theology of the Truth. He imposed his idea of God upon the everlasting Truth. 'In the beginning was the Word. . . .' And that is all there was, and it was enough.

"Now, brothers and sisters, old John was a white man, and the white man has his ways. Oh gracious me, he has his ways. He talks about the Word. He talks through it and around it. He builds upon it with syllables, with prefixes and suffixes and hyphens and accents. He adds and divides and multiplies the Word. And in all of this he subtracts the Truth. And, brothers and sisters, you have come here to live in the white man's world. Now the white man deals in words, and he deals easily, with grace and sleight of hand. And in his presence, here on his own ground, you are as children, mere babes in the woods. You must not mind, for in this you have a certain advantage. A child can listen and learn. The Word is sacred to a child.

"My grandmother was a storyteller; she knew her way around words. She never learned to read and write, but somehow she knew the good of reading and writing; she had learned how to listen and delight. She had learned that in words and in language, and there only, she could have whole and consummate being. She told me stories, and she taught me how to listen. I was a child and I listened. She could neither read nor write, you see, but she taught me how to live among her words, how to listen and delight. 'Storytelling; to utter and to hear . . .' And the simple act of listening is crucial to the concept of language, more crucial even than reading and writing and language in turn is crucial to human society. There is proof of that, I think, in all the histories and prehistories of human experience. When that old Kiowa woman told me stories, I listened with only one ear. I was a child, and I took the words for granted. I did not know what all of them meant, but somehow I held on to them; I remembered them, and I remember them now. The stories were old and dear; they meant a great deal to my grandmother. It was not until she died that I knew how *much* they meant to her. I began to think about it, and then I knew. When she told me those old stories, something strange and good and powerful was going on. I was a child, and that old woman was asking me to come directly into the presence of her mind and spirit; she was taking hold of my imagination, giving me to share in the great fortune of her wonder and delight. She was asking me to go with her to the confrontation of something that was sacred and eternal. It was a timeless, *timeless* thing; nothing of her old age or of my childhood came between us.

"Children have a greater sense of the power and beauty of words than have the rest of us in general. And if that is so, it is because there occurs—or reoccurs—in the mind of every child something like a reflection of all human experience. I have heard that the human fetus corresponds in its development, stage by stage, to the scale of evolution. Surely it is no less reasonable to suppose that the waking mind of a child corresponds in the same way to the whole evolution of human thought and perception.

"In the white man's world, language, too—and the way in which the white man thinks of it—has undergone a process of change. The white man takes such things as words and literatures for granted, as indeed he must, for nothing in his world is so commonplace. On every side of him there are words by the millions, an unending succession of pamphlets and papers, letters and books, bills and bulletins, commentaries and conversations. He has diluted and multiplied the Word, and words have begun to close in upon him. He is sated and insensitive; his regard for language—for the Word itself—as an instrument of creation has diminished nearly to the point of no return. It may be that he will perish by the Word.

"But it was not always so with him, and it is not so with you. Consider for a moment that old Kiowa woman, my grandmother, whose use of language was confined to speech. And be assured that her regard for words was always keen in proportion as she depended upon them. You see, for her words were medicine; they were magic and invisible. They came from nothing into sound and meaning. They were beyond price; they could neither be bought nor sold. And she never threw words away.

"My grandmother used to tell me the story of Tai-me, of how Tai-me came to the Kiowas. The Kiowas were a sun dance culture, and Tai-me was their sun dance doll, their most sacred fetish; no medicine was ever more powerful. There is a story about the coming of Tai-me. This is what my grandmother told me:

Long ago there were bad times. The Kiowas were hungry and there was no food. There was a man who heard his children cry from hunger, and he began to search for food. He walked four days and became very weak. On the fourth day he came to a great canyon. Suddenly there was thunder and lightning. A Voice spoke to him and said, "Why are you following me? What do you want?" The man was afraid. The thing standing before him had the feet of a deer, and its body was covered with feathers. The man answered that the Kiowas were hungry. "Take me with you," the Voice said, "and I will give you whatever you want." From that day Tai-me has belonged to the Kiowas.

"Do you see? There, far off in the darkness, something happened. Do you see? Far, far away in the nothingness something happened. There was a voice, a sound, a word—and everything began. The story of the coming of Tai-me has existed for hundreds of years by word of mouth. It represents the oldest and best idea that man has of himself. It represents a very rich literature, which, because it was never written down, was always but one generation from extinction. But for the same reason it was cherished and revered. I could see that reverence in my grandmother's eyes, and I could hear it in her voice. It was that, I think, that old Saint John had in mind when he said, 'In the beginning was the Word. . . .' But he went on. He went on to lay a scheme about the Word. He could find no satisfaction in the simple fact that the Word was; he had to account for it, not in terms of that sudden and profound insight, which must have devastated him at once, but in terms of the moment afterward, which was irrelevant and remote; not in terms of his imagination, but only in terms of his prejudice.

"Say this: 'In the beginning was the Word. . . .' There was nothing. There was *nothing!* Darkness. There was darkness, and there was no end to it. You look up sometimes in the night and there are stars; you can see all the way to the stars. And you begin to know the universe, how awful and great it is. The stars lie out against the sky and do not fill it. A single star, flickering out in the universe, is enough to fill the mind, but it is nothing in the night sky. The darkness looms around it. The darkness flows among the stars, and beyond them forever. In the beginning that is how it was, but there were no stars. There was only the dark infinity in which nothing was. And something happened. At the distance of a star something happened, and everything began. The Word did not come into being, but *it was*. It did not break upon the silence, but *it was older than the silence and the silence was made of it.*

"Old John caught sight of something terrible. The thing standing before him said, 'Why are you following me? What do you want?' And from that day the Word has belonged to us, who have heard it for what it is, who have lived in fear and awe of it. In the Word was the beginning; '*In the beginning was the Word.* . . .'"

The Priest of the Sun appeared to have spent himself. He stepped back from the lectern and hung his head, smiling. In his mind the earth was spinning and the stars rattled around in the heavens. The sun shone, and the moon. Smiling in a kind of transport, the Priest of the Sun stood silent for a time while the congregation waited to be dismissed.

"Good night," he said, at last, "and get yours."

Tosamah, orator, physician, Priest of the Sun, son of Hummingbird, spoke:

"A single knoll rises out of the plain in Oklahoma, north and west of the Wichita range. For my people it is an old landmark, and they gave it the name Rainy Mountain. There, in the south of the continental trough, is the hardest weather in the world. In winter there are blizzards which come down the Williston corridor, bearing hail and sleet. Hot tornadic winds arise in the spring, and in summer the prairie is an anvil's edge. The grass turns brittle and brown, and it cracks beneath your feet. There are green belts along the rivers and creeks, linear groves of hickory and pecan, willow and witch hazel. At a distance in July or August the steaming foliage seems almost to writhe in fire. Great green and yellow grasshoppers are everywhere in the tall grass, popping up like corn to sting the flesh, and tortoises crawl about on the red earth, going nowhere in the plenty of time. Loneliness is there as an aspect of the land. All things in the plain are isolate; there is no confusion of objects in the eye, but *one* hill or *one* tree or *one* man. At the slightest elevation you can see to the end of the world. To look upon that landscape in the early morning, with the sun at your back, is to lose the sense of proportion. Your imagination comes to life, and this, you think, is where Creation was begun.

"I returned to Rainy Mountain in July. My grandmother had died in the spring, and I wanted to be at her grave. She had lived to be very old and at last infirm. Her only living daughter was with her when she died, and I was told that in death her face was that of a child.

"I like to think of her as a child. When she was born, the Kiowas were living the last great moment of their history. For more than a hundred years they had controlled the open range from the Smoky Hill River to the Red, from the headwaters of the Canadian to the fork of the Arkansas and Cimarron. In alliance with the Co-manches, they had ruled the whole of the Southern Plains. War was their sacred business, and they were the finest horsemen the world has ever known. But warfare for the Kiowas was pre-eminently a matter of disposition rather than survival, and they never understood the grim, unrelenting advance of the U.S. Cavalry. When at last, divided and ill-provisioned, they were driven onto the Staked Plain in the cold of autumn, they fell into panic. In Palo Duro Canyon they abandoned their crucial stores to pillage and had nothing then but their lives. In order to save themselves, they surrendered to the soldiers at Fort Sill and were imprisoned in the old stone corral that now stands as a military museum. My grandmother was spared the humiliation of those high gray walls by eight or ten years, but she must have known from birth the affliction of defeat, the dark brooding of old warriors.

"Her name was Aho, and she belonged to the last culture to evolve in North America. Her forebears came down from the high north country nearly three centuries ago. The earliest evidence of their existence places them close to the source of the Yellowstone River in western Montana. They were a mountain people, a mysterious tribe of hunters whose language has never been classified in any major group. In the late seventeenth century they began a long migration to the south and east. It was a journey toward the dawn, and it led to a golden age. Along the way the Kiowas were befriended by the Crows, who gave them the culture and religion of the plains. They acquired horses, and their ancient nomadic spirit was suddenly free of the ground. They acquired Tai-me, the sacred sun dance doll, from that moment the chief object and symbol of their worship, and so shared in the divinity of the sun. Not least, they acquired the sense of destiny, therefore courage and pride. When they entered upon the Southern Plains, they had been transformed. No longer were they slaves to the simple necessity of survival; they were a lordly and dangerous society of fighters and thieves, hunters and priests of the sun. According to their origin myth, they entered the world through a hollow log. From one point of view, their migration was the fruit of an old prophecy, for indeed they emerged from a sunless world.

"I could see that. I followed their ancient way to my grandmother's grave. Though she lived out her long life in the shadow of Rainy Mountain, the immense landscape of the continental interior—all of its seasons and its sounds—lay like memory in her blood. She could tell of the Crows, whom she had never seen, and of the Black Hills, where she had never been. I wanted to see in reality what she had seen more perfectly in the mind's eye.

"I began my pilgrimage on the course of the Yellowstone. There, it seemed to me, was the top of the world, a region of deep lakes and dark timber, canyons and waterfalls. But, beautiful as it is, one might have the sense of confinement there. The skyline in all directions is close at hand, the high wall of the woods and deep cleavages of shade. There is a perfect freedom in the mountains, but it belongs to the eagle and the elk, the badger and the bear. The Kiowas reckoned their stature by the distance they could see, and they were bent and blind in the wilderness.

"Descending eastward, the highland meadows are a stairway to the plain. In July the inland slope of the Rockies is luxuriant with flax and buckwheat, stonecrop and larkspur. The earth unfolds and the limit of the land recedes. Clusters of trees, and animals grazing far in the distance, cause the vision to reach away and wonder to build upon the mind. The sun follows a longer course in the day, and the sky is immense beyond all comparison. The great billowing clouds that sail upon it are shadows that move upon the grass and grain like water, dividing light. Farther down, in the land of the Crows and the Blackfeet, the plain is yellow.

Sweet clover takes hold of the hills and bends upon itself to cover and seal the soil. There the Kiowas paused on their way; they had come to the place where they must change their lives. The sun is at home on the plains. Precisely there does it have the certain character of a god. When the Kiowas came to the land of the Crows, they could see the dark lees of the hills at dawn across the Bighorn River, the profusion of light on the grain shelves, the oldest deity ranging after the solstices. Not yet would they veer south to the caldron of the land that lay below; they must wean their blood from the northern winter and hold the mountains a while longer in their view. They bore Tai-me in procession to the east.

"A dark mist lay over the Black Hills, and the land was like iron. At the top of a ridge I caught sight of Devils Tower—the uppermost extremity of it, like a file's end on the gray sky—and then it fell away behind the land. I was a long time then in coming upon it, and I did not see it again until I saw it whole, suddenly there across the valley, as if in the birth of time the core of the earth had broken through its crust and the motion of the world was begun. It stands in motion, like certain timeless trees that aspire too much into the sky, and imposes an illusion on the land. There are things in nature which engender an awful quiet in the heart of man; Devils Tower is one of them. Man must account for it. He must never fail to explain such a thing to himself, or else he is estranged forever from the universe. Two centuries ago, because they could not do otherwise, the Kiowas made a legend at the base of the rock. My grandmother said:

Eight children were there at play, seven sisters and their brother. Suddenly the boy was struck dumb; he trembled and began to run upon his hands and feet. His fingers became claws, and his body was covered with fur. There was a bear where the boy had been. The sisters were terrified; they ran, and the bear after them. They came to the stump of a great tree, and the tree spoke to them. It bade them climb upon it, and as they did so it began to rise into the air. The bear came to kill them, but they were just beyond its reach. It reared against the tree and scored the bark all around with its claws.

The seven sisters were borne into the sky, and they became the stars of the Big Dipper.

"From that moment, and so long as the legend lives, the Kiowas have kinsmen in the night sky. Whatever they were in the mountains, they could be no more. However tenuous their well-being, however much they had suffered and would suffer again, they had found a way out of the wilderness.

"The first man among them to stand on the edge of the Great Plains saw farther over land than he had ever seen before. There is something about the heart of the continent that resides always in the end of vision, some essence of the sun and wind. That man knew the possible quest. There was nothing to prevent his going out; he could enter upon the land and be alive, could bear at once the great hot weight of its silence. In a sense the question of survival had never been more imminent, for no land is more the measure of human strength. But neither had wonder been more accessible to the mind nor destiny to the will.

"My grandmother had a reverence for the sun, a certain holy regard which now is all but gone out of mankind. There was a wariness in her, and an ancient awe. She was a Christian in her later years, but she had come a long way about, and she never forgot her birthright. As a child, she had been to the sun dances; she had taken part in that annual rite, and by it she had learned the restoration of her people in the presence of Tai-me. She was about seven years old when the last Kiowa sun dance was held in 1887 on the Washita River above Rainy Mountain Creek. The buffalo were gone. In order to consummate the ancient sacrifice—to impale the head of a buffalo bull upon the Tai-me tree—a delegation of old men journeyed into Texas, there to beg and barter for an animal from the Goodnight herd. She was ten when the Kiowas came together for the last time as a living sun dance culture. They could find no buffalo; they had to hang an old hide from the sacred tree. That summer was known to my grandmother as Ä'poto Etódă-de K'ádó, Sun Dance When the Forked Poles Were Left Standing, and it is entered in the Kiowa calendars as the figure of a tree standing outside the unfinished framework of a medicine lodge.

Before the dance could begin, a company of armed soldiers rode out from Fort Sill under orders to disperse the tribe. Forbidden without cause the essential act of their faith, having seen the wild herds slaughtered and left to rot upon the ground, the Kiowas backed away forever from the tree. That was July 20, 1890, at the great bend of the Washita. My grandmother was there. Without bitterness, and for as long as she lived, she bore a vision of deicide.

"Now that I can have her only in memory, I see my grandmother in the several postures that were peculiar to her: standing at the wood stove on a winter morning and turning meat in a great iron skillet; sitting at the south window, bent above her beadwork, and afterward, when her vision failed, looking down for a long time into the fold of her hands; going out upon a cane, very slowly as she did when the weight of age came upon her; praying. I remember her most often at prayer. She made long, rambling prayers out of suffering and hope, having seen many things. I was never sure that I had the right to hear, so exclusive were they of all mere custom and company. The last time I saw her, she prayed standing by the side of her bed at night, naked to the waist, the light of a kerosene lamp moving upon her dark skin. Her long black hair, always drawn and braided in the day, lay upon her shoulders and against her breasts like a shawl. I did not always understand her prayers; I believe they were made of an older language than that of ordinary speech. There was something inherently sad in the sound, some slight hesitation upon the syllables of sorrow. She began in a high and descending pitch, exhausting her breath to silence; then again and again—and always the same intensity of effort, of something that is, and is not, like urgency in the human voice. Transported so in the dim and dancing light among the shadows of her room, she seemed beyond the reach of time, as if age could not lay hold of her. But that was illusion; I think I knew then that I should not see her again.

"Houses are like sentinels in the plain, old keepers of the weather watch. There, in a very little while, wood takes on the appearance of great age. All colors soon wear away in the wind and rain, and then the wood is burned gray and the grain appears and the nails turn red with rust. The windowpanes are black and opaque; you imagine there is nothing within, and indeed there are many ghosts, bones given up to the land. They stand here and there against the sky, and you approach them for a longer time than you expect. They belong in the distance; it is their domain.

"My grandmother lived in a house near the place where Rainy Mountain Creek runs into the Washita River. Once there was a lot of sound in the house, a lot of coming and going, feasting and talk. The summers there were full of excitement and reunion. The Kiowas are a summer people; they abide the cold and keep to themselves, but when the season turns and the land becomes warm and vital they cannot hold still; an old love of going returns upon them. The old people have a fine sense of pageantry and a wonderful notion of decorum. The aged visitors who came to my grandmother's house when I was a child were men of immense character, full of wisdom and disdain. They dealt in a kind of infallible quiet and gave but one face away; it was enough. They were made of lean and leather, and they bore themselves upright. They wore great black hats and bright ample shirts that shook in the wind. They rubbed fat upon their hair and wound their braids with strips of colored cloth. Some of them painted their faces and carried the scars of old and cherished enmities. They were an old council of war lords, come to remind and be reminded of who they were. Their wives and daughters served them well. The women might indulge themselves; gossip was at once the mark and compensation of their servitude. They made loud and elaborate talk among themselves, full of jest and gesture, fright and false alarm. They went abroad in fringed and flowered shawls, bright beadwork and German silver. They were at home in the kitchen, and they prepared meals that were banquets.

"There were frequent prayer meetings, and great nocturnal feasts. When I was a child, I played with my cousins outside, where the lamplight fell upon the ground and the singing of the old people rose up around us and carried away into the darkness. There were a lot of good things to eat, a lot of laughter and surprise. And afterward, when the quiet returned, I lay down with my grandmother and could hear the frogs away by the river and feel the motion of the air.

"Now there is a funeral silence in the rooms, the endless wake of some final word. The walls have closed in upon my grandmother's house. When I returned to it in mourning, I saw for the first time in my life how small it was. It was late at night, and there was a white moon, nearly full. I sat for a long time on the stone steps by the kitchen door. From there I could see out across the land; I could see the long row of trees by the creek, the low light upon the rolling plains, and the stars of the Big Dipper. Once I looked at the moon and caught sight of a strange thing. A cricket had perched upon the handrail, only a few inches away from me. My line of vision was such that the creature filled the moon like a fossil. It had gone there, I thought, to live and die, for there of all places was its small definition made whole and eternal. A warm wind rose up and purled like the longing within me.

"The next morning I awoke at dawn and went out of my grandmother's house to the scaffold of the well that stands near the arbor. There was a stillness all around, and night lay still upon the pecan groves away by the river. The sun rose out of the ground, powerless for a long time to burn the air away, dim and nearly cold like the moon. The orange arc grew upon the land, curving out and downward to an impossible diameter. It must not go on, I thought, and I began to be afraid; then the air dissolved and the sun backed away. But for a moment I had seen to the center of the world's being. Every day in the plains proceeds from that strange eclipse.

"I went out on the dirt road to Rainy Mountain. It was already hot, and the grasshoppers began to fill the air. Still, it was early in the morning, and birds sang out of the shadows. The long yellow grass on the mountain shone in the bright light, and a scissortail hied above the land. There, where it ought to be, at the end of a long and legendary way, was my grandmother's grave. She had at last succeeded to that holy ground. Here and there on the dark stones were the dear ancestral names. Looking back once, I saw the mountain and came away."

JAMES WELCH

After Momaday the next Indian writer to achieve prominence was James Welch, whose first novel, *Winter in the Blood*, appeared in 1974. Welch, who is Blackfeet and Gros Ventre, writes primarily about his native Montana. His novels—*The Death of Jim Loney* (1979) and *Fools Crow* (1986) followed *Winter in the Blood*—and his collection of poems, *Riding the Earthboy 40* (1975), do much the same thing for the Milk River Valley and Montana that Faulkner did for Jefferson County and Mississippi. They describe the setting, the people, the history, and the myths of a part of the country that is too remote from urban centers to be known to most Americans but that is nonetheless vital to our history, mythology, and sense of ourselves.

Welch was born in 1940 in Browning, Montana, a town of two thousand on the high plains just outside Glacier National Park that serves as the center of the Blackfeet reservation. He attended schools on the Blackfeet and Fort Belknap reservations, Fort Belknap being the home of the Gros Ventres, his mother's people. He attended the University of Minnesota and Northern Montana College before graduating from the University of Montana. Welch has taught creative writing at the University of Montana, and now teaches Indian literature one semester a year at Cornell, living the rest of the time in Missoula.

"The Marriage of White Man's Dog" is taken from two chapters of *Fools Crow*, a novel about the Blackfeet, or Pikunis, at the last moment in their history that they were able to live as a sovereign people—just before they made peace with the cavalry and settled down (with great misgivings) to become Montanans, Americans. The novel is elegiac, but it ends on a note of hope and assertion, not tragedy.

The novel, a *Bildungsroman,* is the story of the coming of age of the hero, Fools Crow. What Welch portrays very clearly is that although there were dramatic differences between the Blackfeet and the whites who were pouring into their territory, there were also important similarities. Though measured differently, status, wealth, and property were as important to the Blackfeet in the 1860s as they are to white Americans in the 1990s.

In the novel, the hero develops from White Man's Dog, a callow, insecure youth called derisively "dog-lover" by his peers because he has so little to offer women, to Fools Crow, a mature warrior, husband, and tribal leader. In "The Marriage of White Man's Dog," Welch explores the role of religion, ritual, and what whites would consider the supernatural in Blackfeet life. The selection describes the courtship and marriage of White Man's Dog and Red Paint, the Sun Dance that White Man's Dog performs to fulfill a vow, and the dreamlike affair he has with Kills-close-to-the-lake, his father's youngest wife.

The Marriage of White Man's Dog

White Man's Dog had settled down into the routine of the winter camp but there were days when he longed to travel, to experience the excitement of entering enemy country. Sometimes he even thought of looking for Yellow Kidney. In some ways he felt responsible, at least partially so, for the horse-taker's disappearance.[1] When he slept he tried to will himself to dream about Yellow Kidney. Once he dreamed about Red Old Man's Butte and the war lodge there, but Yellow Kidney was not in it. The country between the Two Medicine River and the Crow camp on the Bighorn was as vast as the sky, and to try to find one man, without a sign, would be impossible. And so he waited for a sign.

In the meantime, he hunted. Most of the blackhorn herds had gone south, but enough remained to keep the hunters busy. It was during this season that the hides were prime, and the big cows brought particularly high prices. Very few of the men possessed the many-shots gun, so they hunted with bows and arrows. Their muskets were unwieldy, sometimes they misfired, and always they had to stop the chase to reload. Every man was determined to pile up as many robes as he could in order to buy a many-shots gun the following spring. It was rumored that the traders were bringing wagonloads of the new guns.

Most of the time White Man's Dog hunted with Rides-at-the-door and Running Fisher and a couple of his father's friends.[2] Because the many-shots gun was so scarce, not even Rides-at-the-door possessed one, but the hunting group had grown adept at

1. Yellow Kidney is Red Paint's father. On a recent horse-stealing expedition he was captured by the Crows because of the reckless behavior of Fast Horse, a friend of White Man's Dog's.
2. Rides-at-the-door and Running Fisher are White Man's Dog's father and younger brother.

surprising the blackhorns, riding down on them and among them and getting off their killing shots. They kept Double Strike Woman, Striped Face and Kills-close-to-the-lake busy tanning the hides.[3] Once in a while, White Man's Dog would go off by himself to hunt nearer the Backbone.[4] On those occasions he spent much of his time staring off at the mountains. He longed to cross over them to see what he might encounter, but the high jagged peaks and deep snow frightened him. There were no blackhorns in that country, but there were many bighorns and long-legs. Once he came upon two long-legs who had locked antlers during a fight and were starving to death. Both animals were on their knees, their tongues hanging out of their mouths. Although they were large animals, their haunches had grown bony and their ribs stuck out. White Man's Dog felt great pity for the once-proud bulls. He got down from his horse and walked up to them. They were too weak to lift their heads. He drove an arrow into each bull's heart and soon their heads dropped and their eyes lost depth. He did not even think to dig out their canine teeth, which were much valued as decorations for dresses. As he climbed on his gray horse, he thought of next summer when these bulls would be just bones, their antlers still locked together. He went home without killing anything more that day.

But he killed many animals on his solitary hunts and he left many of them outside the lodge of Heavy Shield Woman.[5] Sometimes he left a whole blackhorn there, for only the blackhorn could provide for all the needs of a family. Although the women possessed kettles and steel knives, they still preferred to make spoons and dippers out of the horns of the blackhorn. They used the hair of the head and beard to make braided halters and bridles and soft-padded saddles. They used the hoofs to make rattles or glue, and the tails to swat flies. And they dressed the dehaired skins to make lodge covers and linings and clothes and winding cloths. Without

3. Double Strike Woman is Rides-at-the-door's first wife and White Man's Dog's mother; Striped Face is Rides-at-the-door's second wife.
4. The Rocky Mountains.
5. Yellow Kidney's wife and Red Paint's mother.

the blackhorn, the Pikunis would be as sad as the little bigmouths who howled all night.

Because there were always dogs lurking about, White Man's Dog would halloo the lodge and then turn and ride off. Once, Red Paint emerged before he could get away, and he stammered something about meat and galloped his horse clear out of camp. But he had looked on her, and afterward her vision came frequently. Sometimes when he imagined himself in his own lodge, her face would float across the fire from him. She was almost a woman and he didn't know when this had happened. It seemed less than a moon ago she had been a skinny child helping her mother gather firewood or dig turnips; now, her eyes and mouth had begun to soften into those of a young woman and her dress seemed to ride more comfortably on her shoulders and hips. Except for that one time she had surprised him, White Man's Dog observed her only from a distance. He had acted foolish and he knew she would scorn him.

One day while he stood on the edge of camp watching the children slide down a long hill on their blackhorn-rib sleds, he had the uncomfortable feeling that he too was being watched. For an instant he thought it might be Red Paint, but when he looked up the hill behind him he saw Fast Horse, arms folded, near the brow. They had not talked much since returning from the raid, had rarely sought each other out. On the few occasions they did get together, Fast Horse seemed sullen. He no longer made jokes at White Man's Dog's expense; he no longer joked with anybody. He didn't brag about his buffalo-runner or flirt with the girls. He didn't hunt with the others and he tended his horses poorly, allowing them to wander a good distance from camp. Most of the time the day-riders would bring them back, but once seven of them disappeared and Fast Horse accepted the loss with a shrug. If the weather was good, he would go off to hunt by himself, seldom returning with meat. When the storms came down from the north, from Cold Maker's house, he would go inside his father's lodge and sulk.[6]

6. The tribe refers to winter as Cold Maker.

His father, Boss Ribs, keeper of the Beaver Medicine, often asked White Man's Dog to talk to Fast Horse, to try to learn the nature of this mysterious illness. Boss Ribs was sure that a bad spirit had entered his son's body. But Fast Horse would have little to do with his friend. Once White Man's Dog almost told Boss Ribs of his son's dream of Cold Maker, but to tell another's dream could make one's own medicine go bad, so he held his tongue.[7] But it troubled him that Fast Horse had not made good on his vow to Cold Maker. The helping-to-eat moon was nearly over and Fast Horse had not yet acquired the prime blackhorn hides for Cold Maker's daughters. To break this vow was unthinkable; it could make things hard for all the Pikunis. But White Man's Dog had another reason for wanting the vow honored. It had come to him one night while lying in bed listening to the wind blow snow against the lodge. Perhaps Cold Maker, not the Crows, held Yellow Kidney prisoner. Perhaps he was waiting for the vow to be fulfilled before he would set the warrior free.

The next day White Man's Dog caught up with Fast Horse just as the young man was starting out on a hunt.

"Fast Horse, I would like to talk."

Fast Horse glanced at him. A fog had come down during the night and the air was gray between them. "Hurry, then. You see I am off to hunt."

"That night you caught up with us at Woman Don't Walk—you told us about a vow you made to Cold Maker."

Fast Horse looked away toward the Backbone.

"You vowed two hides. And you vowed the red coals for the eyes of his daughters. Because of these vows you said he spared your life."

"You stop me to tell me what I already know?"

"I have come to tell you to fulfill your vows. The helping-to-eat moon is passing and soon it will be too late. If a vow—"

Fast Horse laughed. "So you think I am incapable of keeping

7. Fast Horse had dreamed that Cold Maker promised the Pikuni raiders success against the Crows if they would move a rock blocking his ice spring.

my word. You think Fast Horse has become a weakling, without honor."

"No, no! But I wish to hunt with you. I would like to help you acquire the hides." White Man's Dog hesitated, but he knew he would have to go on. "You see, I have it in my mind that Cold Maker holds Yellow Kidney prisoner and will not let him go until this vow is fulfilled. It is your failure that keeps Yellow Kidney from his people."

The look on Fast Horse's face almost frightened White Man's Dog. It was a look of hatred, cold and complete. For an instant White Man's Dog thought of taking back his words. But then he saw another look come into the eyes, a combination of fear and hopelessness, and he knew he had been right to confront his friend.

"I will get the blackhorns. I do not need you—or anybody. I am a man and have done no wrong." Fast Horse kicked the buffalo-runner he had acquired from the Crows in the ribs and led the two packhorses away from camp.

As White Man's Dog watched him ride away, he knew there was something going on inside of Fast Horse that he didn't understand. But it had to do with something other than his vow to Cold Maker. It had to do with Yellow Kidney.

White Man's Dog had given five of his best horses to Mik-api upon returning from the Crow raid. They had sweated together and prayed together, thanking the Above Ones for the young man's return. White Man's Dog thanked Mik-api and gave him a horsehair bridle he had made the previous winter. He left the old man's lodge feeling pure and strong.

But he was back the next day, this time with some real-meat that his mother had given him. The two men ate and talked, and then White Man's Dog left. But he came back often, always with food, for he had never seen any provisions in the old many-faces man's lodge. Mik-api lived alone on the edge of camp and received few visitors. He performed healing ceremonies throughout the winter, elaborate ceremonies to drive out the bad spirits, and White

Man's Dog grew fascinated with his powers. He had never paid much attention to heavy-singers-for-the-sick. Their way seemed like magic to him, and he was fearful to learn too much. But sometimes as he and Mik-api talked, the old man would mix up his medicines or sort through his powerful objects and White Man's Dog did not see much to be afraid of.

One day Mik-api asked White Man's Dog to prepare the sweat lodge, and that was the beginning of the young man's apprenticeship. As he repaired the willow frame and pulled the blackened hides in place, he thought of his actions as a favor to Mik-api. He built up a great fire and rolled the stones into the hot coals. He carried a kettle of water into the sweat lodge. He added more wood to the fire. He felt strong and important, and he was glad to help the old man.

When Mik-api and his patient, a large middle-age man with yellow skin, were settled in the sweat lodge, White Man's Dog carried the large stones with a forked stick into the lodge. He set them, one by one, into a rock-lined depression in the center. Then he stood outside and listened to the water explode with a hiss as the many-faces man flicked it on the stones with his blackhorn-tail swab.

Sometimes Mik-api would go into the sweat lodge alone to purify himself when he had to go to a person who was gravely ill. White Man's Dog would hold Mik-api's robe while listening to the old man sing and pray. He was always surprised at how thin and pale Mik-api was. He always reminded himself that he would have to bring even more meat next time. He had taken to accompanying Mik-api to the sick person's lodge, carrying the healing paraphernalia. Mik-api would clear the lodge and step inside. White Man's Dog would wait outside for as long as he could, listening to the singing, the prayers, the rattles and the eagle-bone whistle. Often these healings took all day, sometimes more. Eventually, White Man's Dog would go to his father's lodge to eat or nap, but he would come back to see if Mik-api needed anything.

Later, in Mik-api's lodge, as he tended the fire, White Man's Dog would watch the frail old man sleep his fitful sleep and wonder at his power. But the young man had no thought to possess such power. He was just happy to help.

One day while Mik-api was sorting through various pigments he said, "Now that we have changed your luck and you have proven yourself a great thief of Crow horses, you must begin to think of other things." Often Mik-api teased him, so White Man's Dog waited for the joke. And it occurred to him that the others had quit teasing him so unmercifully. He was no longer the victim of jokes, at least not more so than any of the others. No one had called him dog-lover since the raid on the Crows. He hadn't really noticed it until now, but the people seemed to respect him. He felt almost foolish with this knowledge, as though he had grown up and hadn't noticed that his clothes no longer fit him.

And now Mik-api was telling him about a dream he had the night before. "As I slept, Raven came down to me from someplace high in the Backbone of the World. He said it was behind Chief Mountain and there he dwelt with several of his wives and children. One night as they were bedding down he heard a great commotion in the snow beneath their tree, and then he heard a cry that would tear the heart out of the cruelest of the two-leggeds. When Raven looked down in the almost-night, he could see that it was a four-legged, smaller than a sticky-mouth but with longer claws and hair thicker than the oldest wood-biter. The creature looked up at Raven and said, 'Help me, help me, for I have stumbled into one of the Napikwans' traps and now the steel threatens to bite my leg off.'[8] Well, Raven jumped down there and tried to pull the jaws apart, but they wouldn't budge. Then he summoned his wives and children to help, but nothing would make those jaws give." Mik-api stopped and lit his pipe with a fire stick. He leaned back against his backrest and smoked for a while. "Then Raven remembered his old friend Mik-api, and so he came last night and told me of his sorrow. We smoked several pipefuls and finally Raven said, 'I understand you now have a helper who is both strong and true of heart. It will take such a man to release our

8. Napikwan is the Pikuni term for white man.

four-legged brother. My heart breaks to see him so, and his pitiful cries keep my wives awake. If you will send this young man, I will teach him how to use this creature's power, for in truth only the real-bear is a stronger power animal.' Then my brother left, and when I awoke I found this dancing above the fire." Mik-api handed White Man's Dog a pine cone. It was long and oval-shaped and came to a point at one end. "I believe this came from Raven's house up in the Backbone."

White Man's Dog felt the pine cone. It had hairs coming out from under its scales. He had never seen such a pine cone. "How will I find this place?" he said.

Mik-api broke into a smile. "I will tell you," he said.

Red Paint sat outside her mother's lodge in the warm sunshine of midmorning. Her robe, gathered around her legs, was almost too warm. Her shiny hair was loose around her neck, framing a bird-bone and blue-bead choker. Her light, almost yellow eyes were intent on the work before her. She had passed, over the winter, from child to woman with hardly a thought of men, although judging by the frequency with which they rode by her mother's lodge, the young men had thought plenty about her. It was clear that when or if Yellow Kidney returned, he would be besieged with requests to court his daughter. But for now, as she bent over her beadwork, she was concerned with other things. Her mother, Heavy Shield Woman, had become so preoccupied with her role as Medicine Woman at the Sun Dance that she hadn't noticed her two sons were becoming boastful and bullying to their playmates. One Spot had even tried to kill a dog with his bow and arrow. And, too, Red Paint was worried about a provider. Although White Man's Dog still kept them in meat, she felt that one day he would grow weary of this task. Without a hunter, they might have to move on to another band, to the Many Chiefs, to live with her uncle, who had offered to take them in.

She held up the pair of moccasins she had been beading. She had taken up beadwork for other people, particularly young men who had no one to do it for them. She was good and her elaborate patterns were becoming the talk of the camp. In exchange, the young men gave her skins and meat, cloth, and the Napikwans' cooking powder. They brought her many things for her work, they tried to outgive each other, but she paid attention only to their goods. Now she looked for flaws in the pattern on the moccasins. She wanted them to be perfect. They were for her mother to wear at the Sun Dance ceremony. She stretched her neck and allowed her eyes to rest on the figure astride the gray horse moving away from camp in the direction of the Backbone. The white capote that the rider wore blended in with the patches of snow and tan grass. Beyond, the mountains looked like blue metal in the bright light. Red Paint bent once again to her work, sewing the small blue beads with an intensity that made her eyes ache.[9]

"And what about you, young man? Now that you are rich and powerful, it is time for you to take a wife." Mik-api lay just inside the entrance to his lodge. The Lone Eaters[10] had returned the day before to the Two Medicine River from the trading house, and the trip had tired him. The lodge skins were raised and he could see White Man's Dog from where he lay.

White Man's Dog sat just outside in the warm sun, rubbing an oily cloth over his new single-shot. He had been firing it earlier that morning, and he was still in awe of its power and accuracy. On his third shot, he had killed a prairie hen at a hundred paces. When he retrieved it, he found only a tangle of feathers and bone.

"As a heavy-singer-for-the-sick I encounter many people. Sometimes they want my healing, other times just to talk. They think they want me to tell them important things, but most often it's the other way around. Just the other day I was invited into the lodge of my friend Yellow Kidney. In passing he mentioned that he would be forever grateful to you for sharing your kills with his family. I told him that you were now a man and becoming adept in the ways of medicine. I told him you had acquired power much

9. Several months now pass, during which Yellow Kidney returns. He has suffered from smallpox and been mutilated by the Crows.
10. The Blackfeet band of which White Man's Dog is a member.

stronger than that of the other young ones, that you would one day distinguish yourself among our people. Of course, I was joking to cheer the poor man up."

White Man's Dog smiled.

"Then I happened to notice Red Paint, who sat across the lodge engaged in her beadwork, and I mentioned that it was too bad our young women seem to favor these beads over quillwork. Yellow Kidney agreed with me but said Red Paint did it for others in exchange for goods. Then he became very sad and held up his fingerless hands and said that he was worse than useless to his family, that Red Paint would grow up poor and no man would have her."

White Man's Dog turned around to face the old man. Mik-api sucked on his pipe and looked out the entrance at nothing in particular. His eyes crinkled as though he were straining to see something.

"I felt sorry for the poor man and, like a fool, said that I might know somebody who would keep her well. Of course, that person would have to hunt for the whole family now. But now that I think on it, perhaps there is nobody that rich and powerful among the Lone Eaters. Perhaps Yellow Kidney will have to seek out such a person among the Small Brittle Fats or the Hard Topknots.[11] I understand there are among them a few young men rich and powerful enough."

"Would you speak for me, Mik-api?" White Man's Dog heard the voice far away. His heart was too far in his throat for the words to come from him.

"Slow down, you foolish young one. You're getting as bad as me. First, you must go to your father and mother and tell them of your intentions. If they agree, I will talk to Yellow Kidney. But what makes you think Red Paint would want such a fool?"

White Man's Dog suddenly slumped back. He remembered Little Bird Woman, Crow Foot's daughter. But only Double Strike Woman had mentioned her as a possible wife. Perhaps Rides-at-the-door and Crow Foot were not aware of such an

---

11. The Small Brittle Fats and the Hard Topknots are two other Blackfeet bands.

arrangement. Nothing had happened. He had not even spoken to Little Bird Woman. White Man's Dog jumped up. "I will speak with them now, Mik-api. I'll be back."

Double Strike Woman argued that it would be advantageous for the two families to be united; that Little Bird Woman was sought after by many men, young and old; that she was built to bear many children.

"Just think of Crow Foot. Many say he will be the next head chief of the Pikunis. They say he is already more important than Mountain Chief, because Mountain Chief is always on the run."

"I don't mind you wanting to marry off this young man, but next time you will consult with me before you do such a thing." Rides-at-the-door was angry. Most of the time, he left things in the lodge up to his sits-beside-him wife, but he too had been thinking of his son's future. In truth, he had been just as surprised, shocked even, as Double Strike Woman at White Man's Dog's request. He hadn't known of his son's interest in Red Paint. And if he were to be honest with himself, he would have admitted that the idea was not appealing to him, not because of Red Paint but because White Man's Dog would have to provide for the entire family.

"I only want what is best for my son," said Double Strike Woman. "If he were to marry into Crow Foot's family, he would have more opportunities."

"You can see he doesn't want Little Bird Woman. He wants to marry Red Paint. He is a man now."

"And what about Yellow Kidney? He will have to marry Yellow Kidney, too, and support him and that whole family! People will make jokes. People will say, There goes Rides-at-the-door's son, he marries whole families."

"And what about you, my son? Do you think you can take such jokes?"

"They will not joke for long," said White Man's Dog.

Rides-at-the-door studied his son.

Kills-close-to-the-lake looked up from her quillwork. She had been following the conversation intently. In the brief silence, she too studied White Man's Dog. Without thinking about it, she had been anticipating this time when White Man's Dog would leave the lodge. But she couldn't believe it was actually happening. With him gone, there would be nothing left for her. But there had been nothing anyway—only his presence and some vague hope. Now it was all gone.

"Your mother and I give you our permission, son. You may propose a marriage to Red Paint and her family. She is a good young woman and will make you happy."

White Man's Dog sneaked a look at his mother, but she was busy cutting meat. He stood and walked to the entrance. "Thank you," he said. He looked down at Kills-close-to-the-lake, but she was bent over her quillwork. "Thank you," he said again. He ducked out of the lodge and ran all the way to Mik-api's.

Four sleeps later the families got together and exchanged gifts. White Man's Dog gave Yellow Kidney three of his best horses. His father gave Yellow Kidney four horses, three ropes of tobacco and a full headdress he had taken from a Parted Hair.[12] Yellow Kidney gave White Man's Dog four horses and a beaded shirt. He gave Rides-at-the-door five horses and a Napikwan saddle. Double Strike Woman gave Red Paint a pair of white beaded medallions for her hair. She hugged the girl briefly.

Earlier, Rides-at-the-door had presented his new many-shots gun to White Man's Dog. "You're going to have to do a lot of hunting now." White Man's Dog then gave his single-shot to his father. "Between you and Running Fisher, you now have two shots."

White Man's Dog had left nothing to chance. The day before, he had gone to the camp of the Grease Melters[13] to look up a man who specialized in Liars' Medicine. The man constructed two bark figures—a man and a woman—and poured the magic liquid between them. That would ensure good loving. He charged his client a large packhorse he had noticed during the trade.

12. A Sioux Indian.
13. Another Blackfeet band.

Now, on the twenty-third day of the new-grass moon, Red Paint moved her things into the small tipi beside the big lodge of Rides-at-the-door. That night the families and friends feasted on boss ribs and tongues and buffalo hump. One of the men had brought a tin of the white man's water, and the feast soon turned loud and boisterous. White Man's Dog drank the liquor and talked and laughed, but he was a little disappointed that Kills-close-to-the-lake and Mik-api were not there. Mik-api had said, "I am an old man. Celebrations are for the young." White Man's Dog drank some more and laughed louder. Red Paint sat beside him, twirling her feather fan. All the noise made her shy—but more than that, she couldn't believe she was a married woman. Less than seven sleeps ago, marriage had been the furthest thing from her thoughts. She had sought only to help her mother prepare for the Sun Dance. Could it have been only seven sleeps ago that she had touched White Man's Dog's arm and smiled at him? Even then she had no thought that this might happen. And tonight— tonight they would go to their own lodge. She had thought occasionally of what it would be like to lie with a man, but there had been no reality to it. Her mother had said it would happen naturally and it would be good with the right man. Would White Man's Dog be the right man? She glanced at him and his face was shiny with sweat and oil. He sensed her eyes on him and turned. For a moment they looked upon each other; for the first time they looked into each other's eyes. Then Red Paint lowered her eyes to the twirling fan.

White Man's Dog stood and walked outside. He walked away from the lodge and stood in a small field. He smelled the fresh bite of sage grass and looked up at the stars, trying to locate the Seven Persons. His head was fuzzy with the liquor, but he became aware of a small hand on his. "The Seven Persons do not look upon us tonight," he said softly.

"They ride to the west, over there," said a voice that did not sound right to his ears. He turned and looked into the face of Kills-close-to-the-lake. Although she had not been at the feast, she was wearing her elkskin dress and rose medallions in her hair. The sharp sage grass gave way to the scent that made him light-headed.

She said, "I am very happy for you, White Man's Dog. I wish you to have this." And she turned and hurried off into the dark.

He watched her until he couldn't see her anymore. Then he unfurled the object. It was a soft-tanned scabbard for his new rifle. In the faint light of the fire-lit lodges, he could just make out the quillwork thunderbird design. Then the design blurred and he wiped his eyes.

Some time between the moon of flowers and Home Days, with the high hot sun turning the grass from green to pale straw, the Pikuni people began to pack up their camps to begin the four-day journey to Four Persons Butte near the Milk River. Here, the Sacred Vow Woman and her helpers had determined to build a lodge for the Sun Chief, and here they meant to honor him with sacred ceremonies, songs and dances.

Heavy Shield Woman had purchased the Medicine Woman bundle from her predecessor, and her relatives in the camps had procured the sacred bull blackhorn tongues.

On the first day the people assembled near the confluence of the Two Medicine River and Birch Creek. Most of the bands arrived within the compass of the midmorning and midafternoon sun. As each band arrived, members of the All Crazy Dogs, the police society, showed them where to set up. Soon a great circle was formed, as the last of the bands, the Never Laughs, filled the perimeter. The Sacred Vow Woman's lodge was erected in the center and Heavy Shield Woman entered. Then the camp crier rode among the lodges, calling forth all the women who had vowed to come forward to the tongues. He beat his small drum and called for their husbands to accompany them. He stopped before the lodge of Heard-by-both-sides Woman, who had been a Sacred Vow Woman two years earlier, and called her to instruct Heavy Shield Woman in her duties.

When the chosen had been assembled in the lodge, Heard-by-both-sides Woman lifted one of the tongues above her head and asked Sun Chief to affirm that she had been virtuous in all things. All of the women did this. Then the dried tongues were boiled and cut up and placed in parfleches. Heavy Shield Woman began her fast.

The next day she led the procession to the second camp. On her travois she carried the Medicine Woman bundle and the sacred tongues. Four days they camped in four different locations, arriving at last on a flat plain beneath Four Persons Butte. Each day Yellow Kidney and the many-faces man, wise in the ritual of the Sun Dance, purified themselves in the sweat lodge.

The dawn of the fifth day, Low Horn, a celebrated warrior and scout, left his lodge, saddled his buffalo-runner and galloped down off the plain to the valley of the Milk River. As he rode, he examined the big-leaf trees around him. Across the river he spotted one that interested him. It was stout but not too thick. It was true and forked at just the right height. He looked at the tree, the way the sun struck it, and decided it was the chosen one.

When he reached camp—by now everyone was up and the breakfast fires were lit—he rode among the lodges, calling to the men of the Braves society. He ate a chunk of meat while the others saddled their horses. Then he led them back to the spot. Everybody-talks-about-him had been selected to chop it down, and he set upon it with his ax. He had killed many enemies. At midmorning, his bare back shiny with sweat, he gave a final blow and the tree groaned and swayed and toppled into a stand of willows. The men who had been waiting jumped upon the tree and began to slash and hack, cutting off the limbs as though they were the arms and legs of their enemies. Not too long ago, these would have been traditional enemies; now, more than one of the Braves was killing the encroaching Napikwans.

Heavy Shield Woman sat in the Sacred Vow lodge, her face drawn and gray with her fast. Soon it would be over, but the thought of food had become distant and distasteful. She listened to her helpers talk quietly among themselves, but the words were not clear to her ears. She prayed to the Above Ones, to the Below Ones and to the four directions for strength and courage, but each time she began her prayers, her mind drifted and she saw her husband as he had appeared at her lodge door after his long absence. She had greeted him with high feelings, with much crying, hugging and wailing. She was overjoyed to have her man return. But later, as they sat quietly, she had been surprised to feel only pity for him. He was not the strong warrior who had left camp in that moon of the falling leaves. This man was a shadow who looked at her with stone eyes, who no longer showed feelings of love or hate or even warmth. And he had not changed in the ensuing moons. He was no longer a lover, hardly even a father to his children. Was he still a man? Had a bad spirit taken him over? But she, Heavy Shield Woman, had changed too.

Her thoughts were interrupted by the entrance of Heard-by-both-sides Woman and her husband, Ambush Chief. He carried the Medicine Woman bundle and would serve as ceremonial master during the transfer. When all the helpers, clad in gray blankets with red painted stripes, had seated themselves, Ambush Chief began to open the bundle, praying and singing as he did so. The first object he held up was the sacred elkskin dress. He sang of the origin of the garment while the women put the dress on Heavy Shield Woman. Then they draped an elkskin robe over her shoulders. One by one, he removed the sacred objects: the medicine bonnet of weasel skins, feather plumes and a small skin doll stuffed with tobacco seeds and human hair; the sacred digging stick that So-at-sa-ki, Feather Woman, had used to dig turnips when she was married to Morning Star and lived in the sky with him and his parents, Sun Chief and Night Red Light. She and Morning Star had an infant son named Star Boy.

Ambush Chief told of the time So-at-sa-ki, while digging turnips, had dug up the sacred turnip, creating a hole in the sky. She looked down and saw her people, her mother and father, her sister, on the plains and she grew homesick. Night Red Light, upon hearing of her daughter-in-law's act, became angry, for she had warned Feather Woman not to dig up the sacred turnip. Sun Chief, when he returned from his journey, became angry with Morning Star, for he had not kept his wife from doing this, and so he sent Feather Woman back to earth to live with her people. She took Star Boy with her because Sun did not want him in his house. She also took the elkskin dress, the bonnet, the digging stick. She and her son rode down the wolf trail back to her people, and she was happy to be with them. She hugged them and rejoiced, for she was truly glad to be home. But as the sleeps, the moons, went by, she began to miss her husband. Each morning she would watch him rise up. She shunned the company of her mother and father, her sister, even her son, Star Boy. She became obsessed with Morning Star, and soon she began to weep and beg him to take her back. But each morning he would go his own way, and it was not long before Feather Woman died of a broken heart.

As Star Boy began to grow up, a scar appeared on his face. The older he grew, the larger and deeper the scar grew. Soon his friends taunted him and called him Poia, Scar Face, and the girls shunned him. In desperation he went to a many-faces man who gave him directions to Sun Chief's home and whose wife made Scar Face moccasins for his journey. After much traveling, he reached the home of Sun Chief far to the west. Sun had just returned from his long trip across the sky and he was angry with Scar Face for entering his home. Sun Chief decided to kill him, but Night Red Light interceded on behalf of the unlucky young man. Morning Star, not knowing the youth was his son, taught him many things about Sun and Moon, about the many groups of Star People. Once, while on a hunt, seven large birds attacked Morning Star, intending to kill him, but Scar Face got to them first, killing them. When Morning Star told his father of this brave deed, Sun Chief removed the scar and told the youth to return to his people and instruct them to honor him every summer and he would restore their sick to health and cause the growing things and those that fed upon them to grow abundantly. He then gave Poia two raven feathers to wear so that the people would know he came from the Sun. He also gave him the elkskin robe to be worn by a virtuous medicine woman at the time of the ceremony. Star Boy then rode down the wolf trail to earth and instructed the Pikunis in the correct way, and then he returned to Sun's home with a bride. Sun made him a star in the sky. He now rides near to

Morning Star and many people mistake him for his father. That is why he is called Mistake Morning Star. And that is how the Sun ceremony came to be.

While Ambush Chief related this story of Scar Face, three helpers were building an altar near the lodge door. They stripped off the sod and dry-painted Sun, Moon and Morning Star. They painted sun dogs on either side of Sun's face to represent his war paint. Then the helpers chanted and shook their rattles to pay homage to Sun and his family. When they finished, Ambush Chief stood and lifted his face.

"Great Sun! We are your people and we live among all your people of the earth. I now pray to you to grant us abundance in summer and health in winter. Many of our people are sick and many are poor. Pity them that they may live long and have enough to eat. We now honor you as Poia taught our long-ago people. Grant that we may perform our ceremony in the right way. Mother Earth, we pray to you to water the plains so that the grass, the berries, the roots may grow. We pray that you will make the four-leggeds abundant on your breast. Morning Star, be merciful to your people as you were to the one called Scar Face. Give us peace and allow us to live in peace. Sun Chief, bless our children and allow them long lives. May we walk straight and treat our fellow creatures in a merciful way. We ask these things with good hearts."

Before they left the lodge, the helpers with brushes obliterated their dry paintings, just as Sun had removed the scar from Poia.

Red Paint stood next to her husband and watched the procession. The ground was already becoming dusty from the people and horses. Earlier the people had been busy setting up their lodges, getting water from the clear, deep creek that came out of Four Persons Butte, gathering firewood. But now they were all here, watching the procession, moving to the beat of a single small drum. Red Paint was shocked at how old and bent her mother looked. She wasn't even certain that the woman was her mother. Her face was hidden by the hanging weasel skins. Two helpers held her up.

The procession circled halfway around the unfinished Medicine

Lodge. Then they entered a sun shelter to the west of it. Here, the tongues were distributed to the sick, the poor, the children, to all who desired such communion. The women who had vowed to come forward to the tongues opened the parfleches and distributed pieces to the faithful. Heavy Shield Woman, weak from her lack of food, watched the people chew the tongues and she prayed, moving her lips, without words.

It was nearly dark by the time the men of the warrior societies began the task of erecting the center pole of the Medicine Lodge. With long poles they advanced from the four directions, singing to the steady drumbeat. With rawhide lines attached to their poles, they raised the cottonwood log until it stood in the hole dug to receive it. Heavy Shield Woman watched the proceedings with prayers and apprehension, for if it failed to stand straight, she would be accused of not being a virtuous woman. But it did stand, and the men began hurriedly to attach it to posts and poles around the perimeter of the lodge. Younger men began to pile brush and limbs over the structure. Now Heavy Shield Woman sighed and slumped into the arms of two of her assistants. They carried her back to her lodge, where the hot berry soup awaited her. She could break her fast.

For the next four days the weather dancers danced to the beat of rattles against drum. Warriors enacted their most courageous exploits and hung offerings on the center pole. For each deed they placed a stick on the fire until it blazed high night and day. In other lodges Sacred Pipe men and Beaver Medicine men performed their ceremonies for those who sought their help.

All day and into the night, young men in full regalia paraded their horses around the perimeter of the enormous camp. The All Crazy Dogs had a difficult time policing the grounds. But they had discovered none of the white man's water in the encampment, and for that they were grateful. Sometimes they even had time to enter into the stick games that were being played. Throughout the night, the taunting songs of the various sides increased in volume as the stakes grew higher. During the day there were many horse races. Bands raced against each other, societies had their own horses and riders. The betting was heavy and some men lost their entire herds and possessions, even their weapons. Fights broke out over the close races and the All Crazy Dogs moved in, scattering the participants in all directions. And always there were the drums, the singing and dancing.

White Man's Dog awoke at dawn one day with a terrible dread in his heart. He had eaten and drunk nothing the previous day and he could hear his stomach rumble. He sat up in the robes and his body was wet with sweat. The days and even the nights had been hot, but this sweat had nothing to do with heat. He sat up and listened to the steady *thunk! thunk! thunk!* of a single drum. It was the only sound in camp and it was not a call to celebrate but to let the people know where they were.

White Man's Dog looked down at Red Paint. Her loose dark hair fell down around her shoulder. He touched the soft skin. His hand was rough and dark, and it seemed to him that the hand and the shoulder were made of two different substances. He was awed by the power of their lovemaking, and as he looked at her neck and shoulder he was filled with desire. The quiet camp seemed far away to him as he lay back down and reached for and fondled her breasts. He wanted her to wake up and he wanted this dawn to last. But then the thought of the day's ceremony entered his mind and his desire left him.

He stood at the back of the perimeter of lodges and peed. To the east, the first streak of orange crossed the sky. He smelled the prairie grass and the sagebrush and the sweet mustiness of the horses who watched him. He listened to the clear song of the yellow-breast crouched in the grass to his right. Two long-tails flew through the sky toward Four Persons Butte, their black-and-white bodies bobbing lightly through the morning sky. He looked back toward the camp. Most of the outer lodges were unpainted, or had simply painted designs of ocher earth, black sky and yellow constellations. The sacred tipis of Beaver, Blackhorn, Bear and Otter were on the inside of the perimeter, facing the Medicine Lodge. As he watched the sky lighten, the wisps of smoke grew fainter. White Man's Dog stood in the quiet dawn, his heart beating strong with all the power of the Pikunis. He felt ready for the ordeal ahead of him.

Mik-api sat back on his haunches and looked down at White Man's Dog. They were in a brush shelter just to the side of the big Medicine Lodge. The black paint dots trailing from the corners of the young man's eyes glistened in the dappled sunlight. Mik-api looked satisfied. He and two other old men, Chewing Black Bones and Grass Bull, had painted White Man's Dog's body white with double rows of black dots down each arm and leg. On his head they placed a wreath of sage grass and bound the same grass around his wrists and ankles. As the tear paint dried on his cheeks, the old men prayed that he would acquit himself well so that Sun Chief would smile on him in all his undertakings.

Then they led him into the Medicine Lodge and he lay down on a blanket on the north side of the Medicine Pole. He heard a man on the other side recite war honors, and he felt the hands of Mik-api and Grass Bull on his arms. Chewing Black Bones knelt over him with a real-bear claw longer than a man's finger. The man reciting war honors stopped. White Man's Dog looked into Mik-api's eyes and bit his lower lip. He felt the searing pain in his left breast as Chewing Black Bones pierced it with the bear claw. His breathing made a hissing sound in the quiet lodge. Again he felt the claw pierce his flesh, this time on the right breast. His eyes were squinted tight but the tears leaked from them. And now he felt the sarvisberry sticks being pushed under his skin and he looked down and saw the rich blood pouring down onto his arms. Mik-api and Grass Bull helped him up and held him as Chewing Black Bones attached the rawhide lines that hung from the top of the Medicine Pole to the skewers in his breasts.

"Now go to the Medicine Pole and thank Sun Chief for allowing you to fulfill your vow."

White Man's Dog approached the pole and thanked Sun for helping him on his raid and for protecting him. He asked for forgiveness for desiring his father's young wife and he saw Kills-close-to-the-lake that night running from him and he asked her forgiveness too. He felt his head get light and he almost collapsed with pain. He thanked Sun for his fine new wife and vowed to be good and true to all the people. Finally, he asked Sun to give him strength and courage to endure his torture. Then he backed away from the pole and began to dance. He danced to the west, toward the lodge door. He danced to the drum and rattle. From somewhere behind him he heard the bird-bone whistle of a many-faces man, and he felt the sticky warm blood coursing down from his wounds. Then he heard the drum speed up and he danced harder, pulling harder against the lines attached to his breasts. He danced and twisted and pulled and when he thought he couldn't stand the pain the left skewer broke loose, swinging him around to his knees. He bit his lip until he tasted blood mixed with the salty tears running down into his mouth over the black painted tears. He pushed himself up to his feet again and danced to the east, away from the door. He leaned away from the Medicine Pole and jerked his body back and forth, but the second skewer would not give. His head was fuzzy with red and black images and only the pain kept him there in the lodge. Then he saw the dawn and the long-tails and the patient horses. He heard the yellow-breast singing in his ears and then it turned into a voice, loud and deep, and it recited the victories it had gained over its enemies. Raven flew into the lodge and sat down between Red Paint and Kills-close-to-the-lake. One more step, he cawed, think of Skunk Bear, your power—and he felt the other skewer pull free and he fell backward into the darkness.

Mik-api rose and cut the bloody skewers from their rawhide tethers. Small strips of flesh hung from them. He carried them to the Medicine Pole and laid them at the base. "Here is the offering of White Man's Dog," he said. "Now he is for certain a man, and Sun Chief will light his way. His friend Mik-api has spoken to you."

White Man's Dog slept that night by himself a good distance from the encampment of the Pikunis. His wounds were raw and swollen and his stomach had become a small knot, for he had still not eaten. In the distance he could hear the thundering rumble of the drums as the dancing picked up. He lay in his robe on the flat ground and watched Seven Persons and the Lost Children in the night sky. To the east, Night Red Light had risen full over the prairie. Once he saw a star feeding, its long white tail a streak across the blackness.

Then he was dreaming of a river he had never seen before. The waters were white and the sky and ground glistened as though covered with frost. As he watched the white water flow over the white stones, his eye caught a dark shape lying in the white brush. Then he was down beside the water and the wolverine looked up at him with a pitiful look.

"It is good to see you again, brother," he said. "I have got myself caught again and there is no one around but you."

"But why is it so white, Skunk Bear?" White Man's Dog had to shield his eyes from the glare.

"That's the way it is now. All the breathing things are gone— except for us. But hurry, brother, for I feel my strength slipping away."

White Man's Dog released the animal for the second time.

Skunk Bear felt of his parts and said, "All there. For a while, brother, I thought I was a shadow." Then he reached into his parfleche and took out a slender white stone. "For you, brother. You carry that with you when you go into battle, and you sing this song:

> "Wolverine is my brother, from Wolverine I take my
> courage,
> Wolverine is my brother, from Wolverine I take my
> strength,
> Wolverine walks with me.

"You sing that loudly and boldly and you will never want for power."

White Man's Dog watched the wolverine cross the river and amble up the white bluff on the other side. Near the top, the animal turned and called, "I help you because twice you have rescued me from the Napikwans' steel jaws. But you must do one other thing: When you kill the blackhorns, or any of the four-leggeds, you must leave a chunk of liver for Raven, for it was he who guided you to me. He watches out for all his brothers, and that is why we leave part of our kills for him."

"He will be the first to eat of my kills," called White Man's Dog. "Good luck, my brother!" But Skunk Bear had disappeared over the top of the bluff.

As White Man's Dog turned to leave, he saw in the glittering whiteness a figure approaching the river. He became frightened and hid behind a white tree. As the figure passed, he saw it was a young woman dressed in white furs and carrying two water bladders. He watched her dip the bladders into the river until they were full; then she hung them from a branch and took off her furs. She was slender but her breasts and hips were round. She stepped over the stones to the water's edge, arched her back and dove in. She came up and swung her long hair, and White Man's Dog became rigid with desire for her. He wanted his arms around her smooth brown back and he wanted to lay her down in the white grass. As he approached the riverbank, he began to take off his clothes and he heard a song which seemed to come from him. The young woman turned and looked at him. It was Kills-close-to-the-lake. She made no attempt to cover herself.

White Man's Dog quickly turned away.

"Are you afraid of me?"

"No, I am afraid for myself," he said.

"Why? Do you desire me?"

"I can't say. It is not proper."

"Why not? This is the place of dreams. Here, we may desire each other. But not in that other world, for there you are my husband's son."

White Man's Dog looked at her, and he felt nothing but desire. He tried to feel shame, guilt, but these feelings would not come.

"You may desire me, if you wish. Nothing will happen. You may lie with me, if you like." She moved out of the water and stood before him. She looked into his eyes, and he saw Kills-close-to-the-lake for the first time. He saw the hunger she had kept hidden, he saw her beauty, and he saw her spirit.

So they lay down in the white grass together, their bodies warm and alive. He covered her breasts with his hands and pressed his mouth to her slender neck. He smelled her familiar scent and knew it was her. She moved beneath him and pulled him down and he closed his eyes. He felt her fingers tracing words on his back, and then he slept.

White Man's Dog awoke with his cheek against the damp dawn grass. At first he didn't know where he was. He was all alone and it frightened him. He sat up quickly and felt the sudden pain of his chest. He looked down and saw the strip of trade cloth that had been wound around his torso. Beneath the cloth he saw the leaves and the salve, and he remembered the events of the previous day. He was weak with hunger, and he fell back on his elbows. Sun was not yet up, but he saw Morning Star on the eastern horizon and, above him, Mistake Morning Star. He shook his head as though the whiteness of the stars had blinded him or reminded him of another place.

When he awoke the second time, Red Paint was kneeling beside him, his father and mother standing behind her. Red Paint smiled at him and helped him up and held him tenderly to her. Her hair smelled of sweet grass, and he whispered in her ear, "You are my woman, Red Paint, and I will always be your man." He felt her lips move against his cheek but he couldn't make out the words.

He turned and touched his mother, holding her away from the pain. She looked anxiously into his eyes.

"I am proud of you, my son," said Rides-at-the-door. "Mik-api tells me you did not cry out once."

"Mik-api is kind," said White Man's Dog.

Rides-at-the-door laughed and hugged him vigorously. He let out a howl and then he laughed too. As White Man's Dog gathered up his robe, he saw a small object fall out. It was a white stone almost as big around and long as his little finger. He tucked it into the strip of cloth around his chest and caught up with his wife.

LESLIE MARMON SILKO

Leslie Marmon Silko was born in Albuquerque in 1948 and grew up at Laguna, in western New Mexico. She is of Laguna, Mexican, and white ancestry. Silko's great-grandfather was a white surveyor and trader who settled at Laguna in 1872, eventually becoming governor of the pueblo. Leslie graduated from the University of New Mexico with a B.A. in English and stayed on to teach creative writing. She has also taught at the University of Arizona.

Silko's first book was a collection of poems, *Laguna Woman*, published in 1974. She published her novel, *Ceremony*, in 1977.

Like Momaday and Vizenor, Silko blends the traditions of the novel with tribal myths. *Ceremony* is simultaneously a realistic account of a mixed-blood Laguna veteran and a retelling of traditional Laguna tales similar to the European Holy Grail—Wasteland myths.

The two stories in this anthology come from *Storyteller*, a collection published in 1981 that includes fiction, autobiography, myth, poetry, and photographs. "The Man to Send Rain Clouds," about the funeral of an old Laguna man, deals with the blending of cultures and religions and with the syncretic nature of rituals. American Christians are generally unaware of the pagan elements in their religious holidays. Brought up with the Christmas tree and the Easter bunny, they seldom wonder about the origin of these symbols. In Silko's story, the mourners follow traditional Pueblo burial practices, but they also ask the local priest to pour holy water on the grave. Here we see two religious traditions coalesce in one moving ceremony. It is interesting to contrast Silko's serious treatment of the blending of the traditions with Erdrich's spoof of the same subject.

The second piece, "A Geronimo Story," is about the attitudes Indians and whites have toward one another.

They found him under a big cottonwood tree. His Levi jacket and pants were faded light blue so that he had been easy to find. The big cottonwood tree stood apart from a small grove of winterbare cottonwoods which grew in the wide, sandy arroyo. He had been dead for a day or more, and the sheep had wandered and scattered up and down the arroyo. Leon and his brother-in-law, Ken, gathered the sheep and left them in the pen at the sheep camp before they returned to the cottonwood tree. Leon waited under the tree while Ken drove the truck through the deep sand to the edge of the arroyo. He squinted up at the sun and unzipped his jacket—it sure was hot for this time of year. But high and northwest the blue mountains were still in snow. Ken came sliding down the low, crumbling bank about fifty yards down, and he was bringing the red blanket.

Before they wrapped the old man, Leon took a piece of string out of his pocket and tied a small gray feather in the old man's long white hair. Ken gave him the paint. Across the brown wrinkled forehead he drew a streak of white and along the high cheekbones he drew a strip of blue paint. He paused and watched Ken throw pinches of corn meal and pollen into the wind that fluttered the small gray feather. Then Leon painted with yellow under the old man's broad nose, and finally, when he had painted green across the chin, he smiled.

"Send us rain clouds, Grandfather." They laid the bundle in the back of the pickup and covered it with a heavy tarp before they started back to the pueblo.

They turned off the highway onto the sandy pueblo road. Not long after they passed the store and post office they saw Father Paul's car coming toward them. When he recognized their faces he slowed his car and waved for them to stop. The young priest rolled down the car window.

"Did you find old Teofilo?" he asked loudly.

Leon stopped the truck. "Good morning, Father. We were just out to the sheep camp. Everything is O.K. now."

"Thank God for that. Teofilo is a very old man. You really shouldn't allow him to stay at the sheep camp alone."

"No, he won't do that any more now."

"Well, I'm glad you understand. I hope I'll be seeing you at Mass this week—we missed you last Sunday. See if you can get old Teofilo to come with you." The priest smiled and waved at them as they drove away.

Louise and Teresa were waiting. The table was set for lunch, and the coffee was boiling on the black iron stove. Leon looked at Louise and then at Teresa.

"We found him under a cottonwood tree in the big arroyo near sheep camp. I guess he sat down to rest in the shade and never got up again." Leon walked toward the old man's bed. The red plaid shawl had been shaken and spread carefully over the bed, and a new brown flannel shirt and pair of stiff new Levi's were arranged neatly beside the pillow. Louise held the screen door open while Leon and Ken carried in the red blanket. He looked small and shriveled, and after they dressed him in the new shirt and pants he seemed more shrunken.

It was noontime now because the church bells rang the Angelus. They ate the beans with hot bread, and nobody said anything until after Teresa poured the coffee.

Ken stood up and put on his jacket. "I'll see about the gravediggers. Only the top layer of soil is frozen. I think it can be ready before dark."

Leon nodded his head and finished his coffee. After Ken had been gone for a while, the neighbors and clanspeople came quietly to embrace Teofilo's family and to leave food on the table because the gravediggers would come to eat when they were finished.

The sky in the west was full of pale yellow light. Louise stood outside with her hands in the pockets of Leon's green army jacket that was too big for her. The funeral was over, and the old men had taken their candles and medicine bags and were gone. She waited until the body was laid into the pickup before she said anything to Leon. She touched his arm, and he noticed that her hands were still dusty from the corn meal that she had sprinkled around the old man. When she spoke, Leon could not hear her.

"What did you say? I didn't hear you."

"I said that I had been thinking about something."

"About what?"

"About the priest sprinkling holy water for Grandpa. So he won't be thirsty."

Leon stared at the new moccasins that Teofilo had made for the ceremonial dances in the summer. They were nearly hidden by the red blanket. It was getting colder, and the wind pushed gray dust down the narrow pueblo road. The sun was approaching the long mesa where it disappeared during the winter. Louise stood there shivering and watching his face. Then he zipped up his jacket and opened the truck door. "I'll see if he's there."

Ken stopped the pickup at the church, and Leon got out; and then Ken drove down the hill to the graveyard where people were waiting. Leon knocked at the old carved door with its symbols of the Lamb. While he waited he looked up at the twin bells from the king of Spain with the last sunlight pouring around them in their tower.

The priest opened the door and smiled when he saw who it was. "Come in! What brings you here this evening?"

The priest walked toward the kitchen, and Leon stood with his cap in his hand, playing with the earflaps and examining the living room—the brown sofa, the green armchair, and the brass lamp that hung down from the ceiling by links of chain. The priest dragged a chair out of the kitchen and offered it to Leon.

"No thank you, Father. I only came to ask you if you would bring your holy water to the graveyard."

The priest turned away from Leon and looked out the window at the patio full of shadows and the dining-room windows of the nuns' cloister across the patio. The curtains were heavy, and the light from within faintly penetrated; it was impossible to see the nuns inside eating supper. "Why didn't you tell me he was dead? I could have brought the Last Rites anyway."

Leon smiled. "It wasn't necessary, Father."

The priest stared down at his scuffed brown loafers and the worn hem of his cassock. "For a Christian burial it was necessary."

His voice was distant, and Leon thought that his blue eyes looked tired.

"It's O.K. Father, we just want him to have plenty of water."

The priest sank down into the green chair and picked up a glossy missionary magazine. He turned the colored pages full of lepers and pagans without looking at them.

"You know I can't do that, Leon. There should have been the Last Rites and a funeral Mass at the very least."

Leon put on his green cap and pulled the flaps down over his ears. "It's getting late, Father. I've got to go."

When Leon opened the door Father Paul stood up and said, "Wait." He left the room and came back wearing a long brown overcoat. He followed Leon out the door and across the dim churchyard to the adobe steps in front of the church. They both stooped to fit through the low adobe entrance. And when they started down the hill to the graveyard only half of the sun was visible above the mesa.

The priest approached the grave slowly, wondering how they had managed to dig into the frozen ground; and then he remembered that this was New Mexico, and saw the pile of cold loose sand beside the hole. The people stood close to each other with little clouds of steam puffing from their faces. The priest looked at them and saw a pile of jackets, gloves, and scarves in the yellow, dry tumbleweeds that grew in the graveyard. He looked at the red blanket, not sure that Teofilo was so small, wondering if it wasn't some perverse Indian trick—something they did in March to ensure a good harvest—wondering if maybe old Teofilo was actually at sheep camp corraling the sheep for the night. But there he was, facing into a cold dry wind and squinting at the last sunlight, ready to bury a red wool blanket while the faces of his parishioners were in shadow with the last warmth of the sun on their backs.

His fingers were stiff, and it took him a long time to twist the lid off the holy water. Drops of water fell on the red blanket and soaked into dark icy spots. He sprinkled the grave and the water disappeared almost before it touched the dim, cold sand; it reminded him of something—he tried to remember what it was, because he thought if he could remember he might understand this. He sprinkled more water; he shook the container until it was empty, and the water fell through the light from sundown like August rain that fell while the sun was still shining, almost evaporating before it touched the wilted squash flowers.

The wind pulled at the priest's brown Franciscan robe and swirled away the corn meal and pollen that had been sprinkled on the blanket. They lowered the bundle into the ground, and they didn't bother to untie the stiff pieces of new rope that were tied around the ends of the blanket. The sun was gone, and over on the highway the eastbound lane was full of headlights. The priest walked away slowly. Leon watched him climb the hill, and when he had disappeared within the tall, thick walls, Leon turned to look up at the high blue mountains in the deep snow that reflected a faint red light from the west. He felt good because it was finished, and he was happy about the sprinkling of the holy water; now the old man could send them big thunderclouds for sure.

Most of the scouts were at the corral catching their horses and saddling up. I saw them there, busy, getting ready to go; and the feeling of excitement hit me in the stomach. I walked faster. The dust in the first corral was so thick I couldn't see clearly. The horses were running in crowded circles while the men tried to rope them. Whenever someone threw a rope, all the horses would bolt away from it, carrying their heads low. I didn't see our horses. Maybe Mariano thought that me and my uncle weren't going and he left our horses in the pasture.

For a while it had looked like my uncle couldn't go this time because of his foot: he tripped over a big rock one night when he was coming back from the toilet and broke some little bones in his foot. The "sparrow bones" he called them, and he wrapped up his foot in a wide piece of buckskin and wore his moccasins instead of cavalry boots. But when Captain Pratt came to the house the night after they got the message about Geronimo, Siteye shook his head.

"Shit," he said, "these Lagunas can't track Geronimo without me."

Captain said, "O.K."

Siteye sat there staring out the screen door into the early evening light; then he looked at me. "I think I'll bring my nephew along. To saddle my horse for me."

Captain nodded.

The other corral was full of horses: they were standing quietly because nobody was in there trying to catch them. They saw me coming and backed away from me, snorting and crowding each other into the corner of the corral. I saw Rainbow right away. My uncle's horse. A tall, strong horse that my uncle bought from a Mexican at Cubero; my uncle has to have a big horse to carry him. The horses that we raise at Laguna don't get as powerful as

Rainbow; but they eat less. Rainbow always ate twice as much. Like my uncle, Siteye is a big man—tall and really big—not fat though, big like an elk who is fast and strong—big like that. I got the lariat rope ready and stepped inside the corral; the horses crowded themselves into the corners and watched me, probably trying to figure out which one of them I was going to catch. Rainbow was easy to catch; he can't duck his head down as low as the others. He was fat and looked good. I put the bridle on him and led him out the gate, watching, careful to see that one of the others didn't try to sneak out the gate behind us. It was hard to swing the saddle onto his back; Siteye's saddle is a heavy Mexican saddle—I still use it, and even now it seems heavy to me.

The cinch would hardly reach around his belly. "Goddamn it, horse," I told him, "don't swell up your belly for me." I led him around a little to fool him, so he would let the air out, then I tightened the cinch some more. He sighed like horses do when you cinch them up good and they know you've got them. Then, when I was finished, all I had to do was drop the bridle reins, because this horse was specially trained to stand like he was tied up whenever you drop the reins in front of him, and he would never wander away, even to eat. I petted him on the neck before I went to catch my horse. Rainbow was such a beautiful color too—dark brown with long streaks of white on each of his sides—streaks that ran from behind his ears to the edge of his fat flanks. He looked at me with gentle eyes. That's a funny thing about horses—wild and crazy when they are loose in corral together, and so tame when they've got a saddle on them.

My horse was a little horse; he wasn't tall or stout—he was like the old-time Indian horses—that's what my father told me. The kind of horse that can run all day long and not get tired or have to eat much. Best of all he was gold-colored—a dark red-gold color with a white mane and tail. The Navajos had asked twenty dollars for him when they were only asking twelve dollars for their other saddle horses. They wanted cash—gold or silver—no trade. But my mother had a sewing machine—one that some white lady had given her. My mother said it sewed too fast for her, almost ran over her fingers. So we offered them this new sewing machine with silver engraved trimming and a wooden case. They took the sewing machine, and that's how I got my first horse. That day he was hard to catch. He could hide in between the bigger horses and escape my rope. By the time I managed to catch him I could hear Siteye yelling at me from the other corral.

"Andy!" he called, "Andy, where's my horse? We're ready to go."

It was almost noon when we crossed the river below the pueblo and headed southwest. Captain Pratt was up ahead, and Siteye and Sousea were riding beside him. I stayed behind, because I didn't want to get in anyone's way or do anything wrong. We were moving at a steady fast walk. It was late April, and it wasn't too cold or too hot—a good time of year when you can travel all day without any trouble. Siteye stayed up ahead for a long time with Captain, but finally he dropped back to ride with me for a while; maybe he saw that I was riding all by myself. He didn't speak for a long time. We were riding past Crow Mesa when he finally said something.

"We'll stop to eat pretty soon."

"Good," I said, "because I'm hungry." I looked at Siteye. His long, thick hair was beginning to turn white; his thighs weren't as big as they once had been, but he's still strong, I said to myself, he's not old.

"Where are we going?" I asked him again, to make sure.

"Pie Town, north of Datil. Captain says someone there saw Apaches or something."

We rode for a while in silence.

"But I don't think Geronimo is there. He's still at White Mountain."

"Did you tell Captain?"

"I told him, and he agrees with me. Geronimo isn't down there. So we're going down."

But if you already know that Geronimo isn't there," I said, "why do you go down there to look for him?" He just looked at me and smiled.

Siteye reached into his saddle pack and pulled out a sack full of gumdrops and licorice. He took two or three pieces of candy and handed me the bag. The paper sack rattled when I reached into it, and my horse shied away from the noise. I lost my balance and would have fallen off, but Siteye saw and grabbed my left arm to steady me. I dismounted to pick up the bag of candy; only a few pieces had spilled when it fell. I put them in my mouth and held the quivering horse with one hand and rattled the paper bag with the other. After a while he got used to the sound and quit jumping.

"He better quit that," I said to Siteye after we started again. "He can't jump every time you give me a piece of candy."

Siteye shook his head. "Navajo horses. Always shy away from things." He paused. "It will be a beautiful journey for you. The mountains and the rivers. You've never seen them before."

"Maybe next time I come we'll find Geronimo," I said.

"Umm." That's all Siteye said. Just sort of grunted like he didn't agree with me but didn't want to talk about it either.

We stopped below Owl's Rock to eat; Captain had some of the scouts gather wood for a fire, and he pulled a little tin pot out of his big leather saddlebag. He always had tea, Siteye said. No matter where they were or what kind of weather. Siteye handed me a piece of dried deer meat; he motioned with his chin toward Captain.

"See that," he said to me, "I admire him for that. Not like a white man at all; he has plenty of time for some tea."

It was a few years later that I heard how some white people felt about Captain drinking Indian tea and being married to a Laguna woman. "Squaw man." But back then I wondered what Siteye was talking about.

"Only one time when he couldn't have tea for lunch. When Geronimo or some Apache hit that little white settlement near the Mexican border." Siteye paused and reached for the army-issue canteen by my feet. "That was as close as the Apaches ever got. But by the time we got there the people had been dead at least three days. The Apaches were long gone, as people sometimes say."

It was beautiful to hear Siteye talk; his words were careful and thoughtful, but they followed each other smoothly to tell a good story. He would pause to let you get a feeling for the words; and even silence was alive in his stories.

"Wiped out—all of them. Women and children. Left them laying all over the place like sheep when coyotes are finished with them." He paused for a long time and carefully rewrapped the jerky in the cheesecloth and replaced it in the saddle pouch. Then he rolled himself a cigarette and licked the wheat paper slowly, using his lips and tongue.

"It smelled bad. That was the worst of it—the smell."

"What was it like?" I asked him.

"Worse than a dead dog in August," he said, "an oily smell that stuck to you like skunk odor. They even left a dead man in the well so I had to ride back four miles to Salado Creek to take a bath and wash my clothes." He lit the cigarette he'd just rolled and took a little puff into his mouth. "The Ninth Cavalry was there. They wanted Captain to take us scouts and get going right away."

Siteye offered me the Bull Durham pouch and the wheat papers. I took them and started making a cigarette; he watched me closely.

"Too much tobacco," he said, "no wonder yours look like tamales."

I lit the cigarette and Siteye continued.

"The smell was terrible. I went over to Captain and I said, 'Goddamn it, Captain, I have to take a bath. This smell is on me.' He was riding around with his handkerchief over his mouth and nose so he couldn't talk—he just nodded his head. Maybe he wanted to come with us, but he had to stay behind with the other officers who were watching their men dig graves. One of the officers saw us riding away and he yelled at us, but we just kept going because we don't have to listen to white men." There was a silence like Siteye had stopped to think about it again. "When we got back one of the officers came over to me; he was angry. 'Why did you go?' he yelled at me. I said to him, 'That dirty smell was all over us. It was so bad we knew the coyotes would come down from the hills tonight to carry us away—mistaking us for rotten meat.' The officer was very upset—maybe because I mentioned rotten meat, I don't know. Finally he rode away and joined the other officers. By then the dead were all buried and the smell was already fading away. We started on the trail after the Apaches, and it is a good thing that scouts ride up ahead because they all smelled pretty bad—especially the soldiers who touched the dead. 'Don't get down wind from the army.' That's what we said to each other the rest of the week while we hunted Geronimo."

We started to ride again. The sun had moved around past us, and in a few more hours it would be dark. Siteye rode up front to talk to the other scouts and smoke. I watched the country we were riding into: the rocky piñon foothills high above the Acoma mesas. The trail was steep now, and the trees and boulders were too close to the trail. If you didn't watch where you were going, the branches would slap your face. I had never been this far south before. This was Acoma land, and nobody from Laguna would come to hunt here unless he was invited.

The sun disappeared behind the great black mesa we were climbing, but below us, in the wide Acoma valley, the sunlight was bright and yellow on the sandrock mesas. We were riding into the shadows, and I could feel night approaching. We camped in the narrow pass that leads into the malpais country north of the Zuni Mountains.

"Hobble the horses, Andy. We're still close enough that they will try to go home tonight," Siteye told me. "All four feet."

I hobbled them, with each foot tied close to the other so that they could walk slowly or hop but couldn't run. The clearing we camped in had plenty of grass but no water. In the morning there would be water when we reached the springs at Moss-Covered Rock. The horses could make it until then. We ate dried meat and flaky-dry sheets of thin corn-batter bread; we all had tea with Captain. Afterward everyone sat near the fire, because winter still lingered on this high mesa where no green leaves or new grass had appeared. Siteye told me to dig a trench for us, and before we lay down, I buried hot coals under the dirt in the bottom of the trench. I rolled up in my blanket and could feel the warmth beneath me. I lay there and watched the stars for a long time. Siteye was singing a spring song to the stars; it was an old song with words about rivers and oceans in the sky. As I was falling asleep I remember the Milky Way—it was an icy snow river across the sky.

The lava flow stretches for miles north to south; and the distance from east to west is difficult to see. Small pines and piñons live in places where soil has settled on the black rock; in these places there are grasses and shrubs; rabbits and a few deer live there. It is a dark stone ocean with waves and ripples and deep holes. The Navajos believe that the lava is a great pool of blood from a dangerous giant whom the Twin Brothers killed a long time ago.[1] We rode down the edge of the lava on a trail below the sandrock cliffs which rise above the lava; in some places there is barely room for two horses to pass side by side. The black rock holds the warmth of the sun, and the grass and leaves were turning green faster than the plants and bushes of the surrounding country.

When we stopped for lunch we were still traveling along the edge of the lava. I had never walked on it, and there is something about seeing it that makes you want to walk on it—to see how it feels under your feet and to walk in this strange place. I was careful to stay close to the edge, because I know it is easy to lose sight of landmarks and trails. Pretty soon Siteye came. He was walking very slowly and limping with his broken foot. He sat down on a rock beside me.

"Our ancestors have places here," he commented as he looked out over the miles of black rock. "In little caves they left pottery jars full of food and water. These were places to come when somebody was after you." He stood up and started back slowly. "I suppose the water is all gone now," he said, "but the corn might still be good."

When we finally left the lava flow behind us and moved into the foothills of the Zuni Mountains, Siteye looked behind us over the miles of shining black rock. "Yes," he said, "it's a pretty good place. I don't think Geronimo would even travel out there."

Siteye had to ride up front most of the time after we entered the Zuni Mountains. Captain didn't know the trail, and Sousea wasn't

1. The Twin Brothers are heroes in Navajo mythology.

too sure of it. Siteye told me later on he wasn't sure either, but he knew how to figure it out. That night we camped in the high mountains, where the pines are thick and tall. I lay down in my blanket and watched the sky fill with heavy clouds; and later in the night, rain came. It was a light, spring rain that came on the mountain wind. At dawn the rain was gone, and I still felt dry in my blanket. Before we left, Siteye and Captain squatted in the wet mountain dirt, and Siteye drew maps near their feet. He used his forefinger to draw mountains and canyons and trees.

Later on, Siteye told me, "I've only been this way once before. When I was a boy. Younger than you. But in my head, when I close my eyes, I can still see the trees and the boulders and the way the trail goes. Sometimes I don't remember the distance—things are closer or farther than I had remembered them, but the direction is right."

I understood him. Since I was a child my father had taught me, and Siteye had taught me, to remember the way: to remember how the trees look—dead branches or crooked limbs; to look for big rocks and to remember their shape and their color; and if there aren't big rocks, then little ones with pale-green lichens growing on them. To know the trees and rocks all together with the mountains and sky and wildflowers. I closed my eyes and tested my vision of the trail we had traveled so far. I could see the way in my head, and I had a feeling for it too—a feeling for how far the great fallen oak was from Mossy Rock springs.

"Once I couldn't find the trail off Big Bead Mesa. It was getting dark. I knew the place was somewhere nearby; then I saw an old gray snake crawling along a sandy wash. His rattles were yellow brown and chipped off like an old man's toenails." Siteye rearranged his black felt hat and cleared his throat. "I remembered him. He lived in a hole under a twisted tree at the top of the trail. The night was getting chilly, because it was late September. So I figured that he was probably going back to his hole to sleep. I followed him. I was careful not to get too close—that would have offended him, and he might have gotten angry and gone somewhere else just to keep me away from his hole. He took me to the trail." Siteye laughed. "I was just a little kid then, and I was afraid of the dark. I ran all the way down the trail, and I didn't stop until I got to my house."

By sundown we reached Pie Town. It didn't look like Geronimo had been there. The corrals were full of cows and sheep; no buildings had been burned. The windmill was turning slowly, catching golden reflections of the sun on the spinning wheel. Siteye rode up front with Sousea and Captain. They were looking for the army that was supposed to meet us here. I didn't see any army horses, but then I didn't see any horses at all. Then a soldier came out of the two-story house; he greeted Captain and they talked. The soldier pointed toward the big arroyo behind the town.

Captain told us that they were keeping all the horses in a big corral in the arroyo because they expected Geronimo any time. We laughed while we rode down the sloping path into the wide arroyo. Siteye handed me Captain's sorrel mare and Rainbow for me to unsaddle and feed. I filled three gunny-sack feedbags with crushed corn that I found in the barn. I watched them eat: tossing their heads up in the air and shaking the bags to reach the corn. They stood still when it was all gone, and I pulled the feedbags off over their ears. I took the feedbags off the other Laguna horses, then I tossed them all a big pile of hay. In the other half of the corral the Pie Town horses and army mounts had gathered to watch the Laguna horses eat. They watched quietly. It was dark by the time I finished with the horses, and everyone else had already gone up to the big house to eat. The shadows in the arroyo were black and deep. I walked slowly, and I heard a mourning dove calling from the tamarack trees.

They would have good food, I knew that. This place was named for the good pies that one of the women could make. I knocked on the screen door, and inside I could see an old white woman in a red checkered dress; she walked with a limp. She opened the door and pointed toward the kitchen. The scouts were eating in there, except for Captain who was invited to eat with the white people in the dining room. I took a big plate from the end of the table and filled it up with roast meat and beans; on the table there were two plates of hot, fresh bread. There was plenty of coffee, but I didn't see any pies. Siteye finished and pushed his plate aside; he poured himself another cup of coffee.

"Looks like all the white people in this area moved up here from Quemado and Datil. In case Geronimo comes. All crowded together to make their last stand." Siteye laughed at his own joke. "It was some Major Littlecock who sent out the Apache alert. He says he found an Apache campsite near here. He wants us to lead him to Geronimo." Siteye shook his head. "We aren't hunting deer," he said, "we're hunting people. With deer I can say, 'Well, I guess I'll go to Pie Town and hunt deer,' and I can probably find some around here. But with people you must say, 'I want to find these people—I wonder where they might be.'"

Captain came in. He smiled. "We tried to tell him. Both of us."

Siteye nodded his head. "Captain even had me talk to him, and I told him in good English, I said, 'Major, it is so simple. Geronimo isn't even here. He's at White Mountain. They are still hunting meat,' I told him. 'Meat to dry and carry with them this spring.'"

Captain was sitting in the chair beside me. He brought out his tobacco and passed it around the table. We all rolled ourselves a cigarette. For a while nobody said anything; we all sat there smoking and resting our dinner.

Finally Mariano said, "Hey, where are we going to sleep tonight? How about this kitchen?"

"You might eat everything," Siteye answered.

"I think it will be O.K. to sleep in the kitchen," Captain said.

Then Major Littlecock came in. We all stared, and none of us stood up for him; Laguna scouts never did that for anyone. Captain didn't stand up, because he wasn't really in the army either—only some kind of civilian volunteer that they hired because once he had been in their army. Littlecock wasn't young; he was past thirty and his hair was falling out. He was short and pale, and he kept rubbing his fingertips together.

He spoke rapidly. "I will show you the Apache camp in the morning. Then I want you to track them down and send a scout back to lead me to the place. We'll be waiting here on alert." He paused and kept his eyes on the wall above our heads. "I can understand your error concerning Geronimo's location. But we have sophisticated communications—so I couldn't expect you to be aware of Geronimo's movements."

He smiled nervously, then with great effort he examined us. We were wearing our Indian clothes—white cotton pants, calico shirts, and woven Hopi belts. Siteye had his black wide-brim hat, and most of us were wearing moccasins.

"Weren't you boys issued uniforms?" the Major asked.

Siteye answered him. "We wear them in the winter. It's too hot for wool now."

Littlecock looked at Captain. "Our Crow Indian boys preferred their uniforms," he said.

There was silence. It wasn't hostile, but nobody felt like saying anything—I mean, what was there to say? Crow Indian scouts like army uniforms, and Laguna scouts wear them only if it gets cold. Finally Littlecock moved toward the door to leave.

Captain stood up. "I was thinking the men could sleep here in the kitchen, Major. It would be more comfortable for them."

Littlecock's face was pale; he moved slowly. "I regret, Captain, that isn't possible. Army regulations on using civilian quarters— the women," he said, "you know what I mean. Of course, Captain, you're welcome to sleep here." Littlecock smiled, he was looking at all of us: "You boys won't mind sleeping with the horses, will you?"

Siteye looked intently at the Major's face and spoke to him in Laguna. "You are the one who has a desire for horses at night, Major, you sleep with them."

We all started laughing.

Littlecock looked confused. "What did he say, Captain Pratt? Could you translate that for me, please?" His face was red and he looked angry.

Captain was calm. "I'm sorry, Major, but I don't speak the Laguna language very well. I didn't catch the meaning of what Siteye said."

Littlecock knew he was lying. He faced Captain squarely and spoke in a cold voice. "It is very useful to speak the Indian languages fluently, Mr. Pratt. I have mastered Crow and Arapaho,

and I was fluent in Sioux dialects before I was transferred here."
He looked at Siteye, then he left the room.

We got up from the table. Siteye belched loudly and rearranged his hat. Mariano and George reached into the woodbox by the stove and made little toothpicks for themselves out of the kindling chips.

We walked down the arroyo, joking and laughing about sleeping out with the horses instead of inside where the white soldiers were sleeping.

"Remind me not to come back to this place," Mariano said.

"I only came because they pay me," George said, "and next time they won't even be able to pay me to come here."

Siteye cleared his throat. "I am only sorry that the Apaches aren't around here," he said. "I can't think of a better place to wipe out. If we see them tomorrow we'll tell them to come here first."

We were all laughing now, and we felt good saying things like this. "Anybody can act violently—there is nothing to it; but not every person is able to destroy his enemy with words." That's what Siteye always told me, and I respect him.

We built a big fire to sit around. Captain came down later and put his little teapot in the hot coals; for a white man he could talk the Laguna language pretty good, and he liked to listen to the jokes and stories, though he never talked much himself. And Siteye told me once that Captain didn't like to brew his Indian tea around white people. "They don't approve of him being married to an Indian woman and they don't approve of Indian tea, either." Captain drank his tea slowly and kept his eyes on the flames of the fire. A long time after he had finished the tea he stood up slowly. "Sleep good," he said to us, and he rolled up in his big gray Navajo blanket. Siteye rolled himself another cigarette, while I covered the hot coals with sand and laid our blankets on top.

Before I went to sleep I said to Siteye, "You've been hunting Geronimo for a long time, haven't you? And he always gets away."

"Yes," Siteye said, staring up at the stars, "but I always like to think that it's us who get away."

At dawn the next day Major Littlecock took us to his Apache campsite. It was about four miles due west of Pie Town, in the pine forest. The cavalry approached the area with their rifles cocked, and the Major was holding his revolver. We followed them closely.

"Here it is." Littlecock pointed to a corral woven with cedar branches. There was a small hearth with stones around it; that was all.

Siteye and Sousea dismounted and walked around the place without stopping to examine the hearth and without once stopping to kneel down to look at the ground more closely. Siteye finally stopped outside the corral and rolled himself a cigarette; he made it slowly, tapping the wheat paper gently to get just the right distribution of tobacco. I don't think I ever saw him take so long to roll a cigarette. Littlecock had dismounted and was walking back and forth in front of his horse, waiting. Siteye lit the cigarette and took two puffs before he walked over to Captain. He shook his head.

"Some Mexican built himself a sheep camp here, Captain, that's all." Siteye looked at the Major to make certain he would hear. "No Geronimo here, like we said."

Pratt nodded his head.

Littlecock mounted; he had lost, and he knew it. "Accept my apology for this inconvenience, Captain Pratt. I simply did not want to take any chances."

He looked at all of us; his face had a troubled, dissatisfied look; maybe he was wishing for the Sioux country up north, where the land and the people were familiar to him.

Siteye felt the same. If he hadn't killed them all, he could still be up there chasing Sioux; he might have been pretty good at it.

It was still early in the day; the forest smelled green and wet. I got off my horse to let him drink in the little stream. The water was splashing and shining in sunlight that fell through the treetops. I knelt on a mossy rock and felt the water. Cold water—a snow stream. I closed my eyes and I drank it. "Precious and rare," I said to myself, "water that I have not tasted, water that I may never taste again."

The rest of the scouts were standing in the shade discussing something. Siteye walked over to me.

"We'll hunt," he said. "Good deer country down here."

By noontime there were six bucks and a fat doe hanging in the trees near the stream. We ate fresh liver for lunch and afterwards I helped them bone out the meat into thin strips, and Sousea salted it and strung it on a cotton line; he hung it in the sun and started to dry it. We stayed all afternoon, sleeping and talking. Before the sun went down I helped Sousea put the pounds of salted meat strips into gunny sacks and tie them on the kitchen burros, who hardly had anything left to carry. When we got back to Pie Town it had been dark for a long time.

In the morning the white ladies made us a big meal; we took a long time to eat, and it was almost noon before we started northeast again. We went slowly and stopped early so Sousea could hang the meat out to dry for a few hours each day. When we got back to Flower Mountain I could see Laguna on the hill in the distance.

"Here we are again," I said to Siteye.

We stopped. Siteye turned around slowly and looked behind us at the way we had come: the canyons, the mountains, the rivers we had passed. We sat there for a long time remembering the way, the beauty of our journey. Then Siteye shook his head gently. "You know," he said, "that was a long way to go for deer hunting."

GERALD VIZENOR

Gerald Vizenor, a mixed-blood Anishinaabe (Chippewa and Ojibway are the white names for the tribe), was born in Minneapolis in 1934. When Gerald was two his father was murdered by a vagrant, but the police never tried to solve the case. Gerald's uncle died in a mysterious fall from a railroad bridge, and his stepfather fell to his death in an elevator shaft. Throughout his childhood his mother left him with his grandmother on the White Earth Reservation in Minnesota or with foster families.

At fifteen Vizenor lied about his age to get into the National Guard, and as soon as he was able enlisted in the army and shipped out for Japan. There he began to write haiku, and over the years he has published five collections of haiku poems. When Vizenor mustered out he attended NYU and the University of Minnesota. After several tribal and government jobs, Vizenor became a professor, starting at Lake Forest, then moving to Bemidji State, the University of Minnesota, and the University of California at Berkeley and Santa Cruz. He is currently David Burr Professor of Humanities at the University of Oklahoma.

Vizenor published some fiction, essays, and verse during the early seventies, but his big breakthrough as a writer came in 1978 with the publication of *Wordarrows,* a collection of short stories and essays (the distinction between the genres is not always clear in Vizenor's work), and *Darkness in Saint Louis Bearheart,* a novel. These works, with their wild exuberance, their combination of violence and humor, and their innovative use of language, link Vizenor to the postmoderns, writers like Donald Barthelme, Robert Coover, and Stanley Elkin.

Given a childhood filled with violent death and desertion, it is not surprising that Vizenor has a bizarre and bloody view of the universe. However, rather than reacting with bitterness and despair, he fights against the absurdity and injustice of the world with the good-natured élan of the Anishinaabe trickster, Manabozho. Not surprisingly, the trickster is the most important character in Vizenor's works. Vizenor has written three trickster novels, produced a trickster film (*Harold of Orange,* 1983), and written theoretically about the trickster as a linguistic phenomenon (in his collection of critical pieces, *Narrative Chance,* 1989).

Darkness in Saint Louis Bearheart is the first of Vizenor's three trickster novels. In *Bearheart* the trickster archetype is split between two characters, Proude Cedarfair, who represents the figure's positive aspects, and the satyric Benito Saint Plumero, who represents the darker, more irresponsible side.

Vizenor's other two novels feature Griever de Hocus, Vizenor's most important trickster figure, his alter ego. In *Griever: A Monkey King in China* (1987), Griever, like Vizenor a mixed-blood Anishinaabe from White Earth, is a teacher at Chou Enlai University in Tianjin. Vizenor taught in China himself, and a number of Griever's milder adventures actually happened to him. Griever chafes against the authoritarian nature of Chinese existence, causing so much trouble that he finally has to flee for his life. When we last see him he is headed for Macao in a microlight airplane powered by a snowmobile engine. *The Trickster of Liberty* (1988), Vizenor's other Griever novel, fills in some details about Griever's ancestors and childhood but mainly focuses on his trickster siblings.

Our selection, "Luminous Thighs," is Vizenor's first work about Griever. The story, which first appeared in the scholarly journal *Genre* and has had very little circulation, is a loosely connected series of sketches; in some of these Griever dickers with Robert Redford about making a film about a mixed-blood trickster. (Vizenor worked on his film about a mixed-blood trickster at Redford's Sundance Institute.) The epigraphs that precede the story (Vizenor, like Umberto Eco, always piles on the epigraphs) indicate that Vizenor shares Momaday's ideas about the mythic nature of literature. The title refers to the warm and glowing thigh of a cherub carved on a pew in the chapel at King's College, Cambridge.

In part i of "Luminous Thighs," Griever is on a train to Cambridge. He is described as a man who has "learned . . . how to disguise and contrive the common world," who "holds cold reason on a lunge line." These mixed and strained metaphors (what rhetoricians call the trope of catachresis) twist language into strange shapes, and although they are impervious to rational understanding, they are sufficiently powerful and vivid to be understood intuitively.

In part ii we see Griever in King's College Chapel, massaging the mysterious glowing thigh. With him are two Indian women, China Browne and Lettice Swann. In this story China is an "urban tribal mixedblood" whom Griever has met in Berkeley. In the two Griever novels, Vizenor changes China to an Anishinaabe from White Earth who grew up with Griever.

Lettice Swann is a Pottowatomi from Oklahoma. This is an in-joke. Vizenor's chairman at Berkeley, Terry Wilson, whom Vizenor mentions in this story and most of his other works, is a Pottowatomi from Oklahoma, and Vizenor loves to tease him.

The rest of the piece consists of a scene from Griever's film, "Luminous Thighs," a review of the novel *Hanta Yo* and its television adaptation, and some correspondence between Griever and Redford.

It is difficult to classify a piece like "Luminous Thighs" by genre because Vizenor delights in testing the limits of form as well as language. It is difficult to tell his fiction from his nonfiction; both are based on people he knows whose behavior is so bizarre it appears improbable as fact and unrealistic as fiction. Readers may initially find Vizenor obscure and puzzling, but with time and patience they will find he is one of the most enjoyable authors of our time, a modern Rabelais.

Luminous Thighs *Mythic Tropisms*

I believe that all narration, even that of a very ordinary event, is an extension of the stories told by the great myths that explain how this world came into being. . . . Man will never be able to do without listening to stories.—Mircea Eliade, *Ordeal by Labyrinth,* 1983.

Myths can tolerate almost any kind of treatment except indifference or the solicitousness of historical scholarship. . . . Myths can be weakened but hardly annihilated by disbelief; for a successful mythology is one which encourages people to invent new and more reputable reasons for believing in it after the old ones are no longer tenable.—K. K. Ruthven, *Myth,* 1976.

All true mythologies grow. We do not know how or whence. We only know they arise in us as both strange messengers and messages in one.—Sir Laurens van der Post, *The Times,* July 12, 1984.

Language is the main instrument of man's refusal to accept the world as it is. Without that refusal, without the increasing generation by the mind of 'counter worlds' . . . we would turn forever on the treadmill of the present. . . .

   Fiction was disguise: from those seeking out the same water-hole, the same sparse quarry, or meagre sexual chance. To misinform, to utter less than the truth was to gain a vital edge of space or subsistence. Natural selection would favour the contriver. Folk tales and mythology retain a blurred memory of the evolutionary advantage of mask and misdirection. . . . poetic visions, the linguistic capacity to conceal, misinform, leave ambiguous, hypothesize, invent is indispensable to the equilibrium of human consciousness and to the development of man in society. . . .—George Steiner, *After Babel,* 1975.

i   The Intercity Train to Cambridge:

Griever de Hocus learned from various tribal tricksters, from those who misinformed him the most, how to disguise and contrive the common world, an act of survival on the run, and the art of mythic appearances. "Paint the mirrors, break umbrellas," he wrote in *New Myths to The Silk,* an unpublished historical novel, "and reverse the most familiar worlds. Turn your faces out in a cold rain and become a real myth for the night."

Griever moves like an insect in a humid crowd; he leans too close to burnished thighs, pinches elbows. He chooses verbs like toxins for a ceremonial hunt and rolls his head between fast paragraphs. Near the treeline, induced from his imaginative wordfires, he plots new scenes in stories about two writers.

"This novelist had a small car for sale," Griever told an educated man in the opposite seat on the train to Cambridge. The man smiled but held his book while he listened. "When I inquired about the actual mileage he paused, pinched his nose, and said to me: 'Listen mate, mileage is a material illusion, the real world moves in myths and metaphors.'"

"No shit, I said, did you write that in the back seat on the little road to church? I leaned real close and asked him if he had ever dreamed about becoming a woman. Writers understand myths better than preachers, we both knew that much for certain. I kicked the wind checked tires in four directions. Well, later I offered not to tell anyone that he once owned the car. He paused for a moment, pinched his ear, and then he reduced the price."

"How interesting," said the man on the train.

"Not really."

"What ever happened to the car then?"

"Well, that night I drove it into the river."

"The river?"

"The car was still in his name," Griever explained, "and when the number plate was traced there were reports that he had drowned, and that he might have killed himself."

"How cruel," the man said and returned to his book.

"Not really, tired novelists like to discuss their mortal existence at press conferences from time to time, a resurrection, as it were, from their own myths."

Griever slapped his thighs and leaned back in the seat. The train lurched past the narrow rural roads, stories flashed behind the hedgerows. Old words turned in his memories, quaked like leaves that never mend the wind, words that break from their stems before the seasons end.

"King's College Chapel, have you been there?"

Silence.

"Ten years ago I laid my hand on a perfect thigh there, in the back row," Griever announced in a low tone of voice and then he threw his head back against the seat and stared at the ceiling of the coach. "Luminous thigh, never touched one like it since."

Silence.

"Luminous Thighs, how's that for a movie title?"

Griever, a mixedblood tribal trickster born on a reservation in the back seat of a plain brown station wagon, holds cold reason on a lunge line while he imagines the world. His father worked for a circus and his mother grieved, a new meditation practice which she said was a sacred tribal tradition. Griever, conceived in mythic time, is a close relative to the mind monkeys from Asian cultures. He fashions new scenes from interior landscapes with colored pens; he thinks backwards, and stops time like a shaman—or so he claims in casual conversations.

"I can stop time" he announced to the man whose fingers had curved inward in silence; he slumped over his book, asleep in the middle of a compound sentence. His upper lip twitched and his nostrils flared in a wild dream walk to a natural water hole.

"For if animals dream, as they manifestly do," writes George Steiner in *Salmagundi,* "such 'dreams' are generated and experienced outside any linguistic matrix. Their content, their sensory dynamics, precede, are external to, any linguistic code. . . . Language is, in a sense, an attempt to interpret, to narrate dreams older than itself. But as he narrates his dreams, *homo sapiens* advances into contradiction: the animal no longer understands him, and with each narrative-linguistic act, individuation, the break between the ego and the communion of shared images, deepens. Narrated, interpreted, dreams have passed from truth into history."

The trickster advanced to the next coach on the train and sat across from a tall pale woman with small breasts. She wore white shoes with leather tassels. Her lips curved downward and her feet turned inward. She smiled and closed her little book of poems.

"Haiku," she said and presented her book.

"Fat green flies," Griever responded.

"Square dance . . ."

"Histories across the grapefruit," he added.

"Honor your partner," she concluded and clapped her hands to celebrate a haiku. She held a wide smile, her face seemed to separate and her feet turned outward like two thin sheep tethered on a meadow.

"Call me Griever."

"Why?"

"Robert Frost is a liar," Griever announced.

"Never."

"Robert Frost lied," he said and leaned forward. His head bounced from side to side over the rough track. "He never was a swinger of birch trees like he wrote."

"How do you know that?"

"Because, I swing box elder trees . . ."

"So, what does that mean?"

"Well, I was about to say that anybody who has turned down a tree would never write about it the way he did in his poems."

Her thighs closed, the sheep grazed inward.

"Robert Frost, you old birch liar, I said to him at a reading once, but he was much too old to hear me."

"Cruel American," she whispered.

"Frost told the lies, not me," pleaded Griever. When he looked down at her white shoes his mood changed and he wriggled his fingers around his head. "But I do love to tell haikus."

She leaned to one side in rigid silence, retreated into her book, but when the train lurched on a sharp curve she lost her balance. Her head bounced on the rim of the window; her feet leaped free and wagged in space. Her wide white thighs flashed like fish bellies and her pink crotch spread on the rough seat but she never lost her firm grip on that little book of haikus.

ii   King's College Chapel at Cambridge:

These are theories in which literature is seen as the use of mythic forms and others in which it is seen as the recreation of mythic sensibility.—Michael Bell, *Primitivism*, 1972.

Fiction is not discontinuous with reality. Though it deals with shadows, by some magic which can still not be fully explained it can temporarily relieve anxieties and satisfy desires aroused by our actual experience.—Simon Lesser, *Fiction and the Unconscious,* 1957.

Since the environment cannot be authentically engaged the self becomes its own environment and sole source of authenticity, while all else becomes abstract and alien.—John W. Aldridge, *The American Novel and the Way We Live Now,* 1983.

Griever sidled through the King's College Gatehouse like an errant monk but with the wide smile of a trickster. He circled Gibbs' Building past Old Lodge and entered the Chapel from Front Court. Inside, in the cool stone air and rich light, he counted cadence as he weaved between passive tourists and rows and rows of vacant chairs to the organ case screens. There, in the dark wooden vault, he extended his short arms, pitched his shoulders from side to side like a swimmer and turned in a slow circle. With his head back the roses carved on the wooden ceiling turned in the shadows.

Griever was prepared this time, his second visit to Cambridge. Ten years earlier, when he was on a special tour of academic shrines, he encountered two unusual women, China Browne and Lettice Swann, in King's College Chapel.

China Browne stood alone at the end of the Chapel in front of the High Altar and Rubens' *Adoration of the Magi.* Griever asked her to take his picture as he posed like an angel in magical flight, the tips of his golden wings touched and shivered in blurred light, but he did not have a camera. When he read *On Photography* by Susan Sontag he sold his camera and closed his darkroom in the basement. He no longer collects or possesses the world on film, but he does like others to take his picture. China laughed when he borrowed a simple flash camera from a tourist and then asked the woman to mail a print to his academic address. Griever and China posed at the rail for one photograph which was mailed to them, with an invoice for services, several months later.

Lettice Swann was supine on a bench in the back row of the Choir Stalls. She wore bright white shoes with recessive heels; her feet were turned inward even while she rested on her back. Griever reached to touch a carved cherub on the Provost's Desk at the end of the Choir Stalls when he heard a whisper from the back row. He turned and saw her bleached blonde hair spread over the dark wooden bench like the hide of a small animal. Her hands rested on her breasts.

"Touch this one," she whispered and then pointed to a carved statue at the end of the bench on the top row.

Griever stepped over the red rope barrier—tied to control the movement of tourists—mounted the wide carpeted steps, beneath the carved cherubs and satyrs, to the back row of the Choir Stall. There, at the corner, he pressed his moist hand to her sensuous thigh. The muscles on her shoulders and cheeks shivered like a horse down to water. The burnished thigh was warm, turned warmer; the carved androgyne rested on one knee, her head turned low to the right shoulder. His hair was bound forward and plaited loose with cloth. Griever stroked her wide thigh which was thrust to the right in the high window light. His muscular arms pinched her breasts small at the post; one foot extended behind her buttocks, the enormous toes on the other foot, carved into the base of the stall, were broken and worn smooth.

Griever leaned against the dark wooden androgyne and with his right hand he pressed the "play" button on his miniature tape recorder. Turned to full volume the tape crackled twice, hissed, and then the music, recorded by Giovani Gabrieli in King's College Chapel, escaped. The thigh began to glow with the sound of each anthem. At first the tourists took the shallow recorded music into their travels but some of the children were not fooled and in time a crowd of curious men gathered at the red rope to watch a torpid blonde hold her breasts and an ecstatic mixedblood trickster clutch the thigh of a wooden statue.

Lettice dropped her breasts and Griever released his luminous hand from the androgyne when the music stopped, seconds before uniformed officials arrived at the red rope.

"Griever the Carver is my name."

"The Carver family?" questioned one official.

"The Luminous Carver," said Griever.

"You, sir, are the third one this month."

iii   Veronica Moves at Sundance:

The opposite of to love is not to hate but to separate. If love and hate have something in common it is because, in both cases, their energy is that of bringing and holding together—the lover with the loved, the one who hates with the hated. Both passions are tested by separation. . . . Love aims to close all distance. Yet if separation and space were annihilated neither loved one nor lover would exist.—John Berger, *And Our Faces, My Heart, Brief as Photos,* 1984.

Robert Redford
Sundance Film Institute
Provo, Utah

Dear Ordinary Bob:
    We met on your Mandan Ski Lift two summers ago, remember? I'm the one who rode around and around on the chair lift when you were, as usual, three hours late for our appointment. In the end, however, the wait was worth the pleasure of your smile.
    "Luminous Thighs," which you applauded on the lift, appears in several mythic parts. Here it is. Each episode opens with a close focus on the dark wooden thigh of an androgyne statue in King's College Chapel. Those who touch the thigh experience ecstatic heat, symbolic reversals and mythic transformations. I told you on the Mandan that my imaginative stories feature mixedbloods, and so, the characters here are tribal mixedbloods.

LUMINOUS THIGHS
Film Proposal in Two Voices
By Griever de Hocus

Part One: *Gull Shit and Lighthouses*

Lettice Swann stands behind the engraved flowers and lightning bolts on a new window of Saint Nicholas Church at Moreton in Dorset. Her narrow face is pinched behind a black motorcycle helmet. Lettice touches her nose and thick lips to the engraved petals, a perfect distance from Manley Powers, a turf accountant and novice church historian named after a famous general, who is on the other side of the window. She removes her black gloves, knocks on the window, and asks for directions. He comes to attention and smiles, his wide lips waver behind the engraved window. She speaks too loud, her voice breaks.

MANLEY

Wool?

LETTICE

Yes, Wooool, is it near here?

MANLEY

Whatever do you want at Wool?

LETTICE

Lawrence of Arabia.

MANLEY

Yes, of course.

LETTICE

What did you say?

Manley stiffens, raises his head, moves back from the window and expands his stout chest. Lettice, overdressed for a scooter, removes her helmet and enters the little church. Her orange eyes, fusion bombs on an ashen face, flash in the shadows of the altar. Like her father she suffers from low blood pressure and poor circulation; she is drawn to heat, thrills, and fire, like a moth to light. Her doctor told her to be different. "Act like a man," he prescribed. "Deviation will cause you enough trouble to live a long life."

LETTICE

What are you doing here?

MANLEY

You're an American then?

LETTICE

Yes, how can you tell?

MANLEY

Your gloves, really.

LETTICE

My gloves? But I bought them in London.

MANLEY

Well then, who would ever know?

Lettice is nervous; she squints, looks around the church and then examines a thin fissure on the inside of one glove. When she squints her pale cheeks seem to inflate.

MANLEY

New glass, do you like the engraving?

LETTICE

Nice flowers, modern . . .

MANLEY

Modern?

LETTICE

Yes, no colors.

MANLEY

Primitive, I should think.

LETTICE

Listen, this is not primitive.

Lettice is more confident now. She moves closer to the window and touches the engraved petals from the inside. Her fingernails are decorated with various shades of orange, colors of the rising sun, marbled like the end papers in rare books. The colors are absorbed in the glass.

MANLEY

Primitive in the sense that the flowers are neither classical nor religious symbols . . .

LETTICE

Right, me too.

MANLEY

Then we are both primitives.

LETTICE

Not me, I'm an Indian, who are you?

MANLEY

Indian? Red or otherwise?

LETTICE

Pottawatomi from Oklahoma.

MANLEY

I love primitives.

LETTICE

I hate civilization . . . Why am I here?

MANLEY

Looking for Wool?

LETTICE

Where did you say it was?

Manley posed like a general near the last window installed in the village church. Saint Nicholas, located near an old airfield, was bombed during the war. The final window, which replaced the shattered stained panes, was an engraved scene of lightning flashes and two rivers—the Piddle and Frome flow near Moreton. Manley owned a Morgan; he told her to follow close behind.

MANLEY

Lawrence died on a motorcycle not a scooter.

LETTICE

The animals and birds are luminous there.

MANLEY

Luminous where?

LETTICE

Where he died at Wool.

Manley drove fast along the Frome to Wool and the luminous grave of Lawrence of Arabia. Lettice followed on her red scooter and three months later she was married to the turf accountant. Manley, through his unusual connections as a bookmaker, found her a research position with the Lighthouse Authority at Trinity House in London. She mounted her scooter each morning, dressed in colored leathers, for the short ride to Savage Gardens where she compiled data on the bird shit damage to lighthouses.

Lettice studied bird shit stains by day and auras at night; she searched the city for luminous people. Several women glowed about the head when they laughed, but the light failed when they were silent. Then, beneath the railroad tracks at Charing Cross Bridge, she found a frail but luminous man. His dark street friends, such as they were, called him Torcher and some sat with him to read at night. Torcher could roll light between his stiff fingers and flick small beam balls into the air; light escaped from his sleeves and shirt collar.

"Sawney Bean, the cannibal king from Scotland, knew about luminous thighs," Torcher told Lettice, "but I learned how to turn the thigh on whilst I sang in the choir at King's College Chapel. Actually, it was a joint choral with St. John's College. My doctor, you see, told me to be active for low blood pressure. 'Reverse the world,' he said to me, 'act like a woman and your cheeks will turn pink.' So I turned to song and now the light never stops."

A train passed overhead and the abutment trembled. Torcher waited and then leaned back when the train passed. His fingers flashed when he counted, when he gestured; he drew pictures of fantastic animals in the dark air.

"We were singing the anthem 'Give Us The Wings of Faith' when I first rested my hand on the statue. The wood was warm. We sang and my hand slid down to the polished thigh. In the middle of 'O How Glorious' my hand was hot and when I looked down the thigh and my hand were surrounded with a blue light.

"When the organ stopped and the anthem ended the Provost leaned over the rim of the stall and stared at me, his demonic face turned dark red and his cheeks trembled in a silent rage. The little satyr on the canopy above him looked down on me with a great smile. . . . That thigh changed me forever."

Lettice abandoned her research on bird shit, neglected her new husband the turf accountant and gave her whole time to the luminous man. She lived with him beneath Charing Cross Bridge for several weeks.

Lettice practiced the anthems and then she entered King's College Chapel with Torcher and together they sang "O How Glorious," until the thigh was luminous. Lettice felt the light flash in her crotch, on her cheeks. She pretended she was a man.

Manley Powers, meanwhile, remembered vivid episodes of his time with Lettice. He pictured her when he watched horses exercise in a paddock but he could not connect her in calendar time. She disappeared in his memories at the end of each episode, like an animal, separate from his sexual fantasies.

Part Two: *Mystic Warrior on the Ropes*

China Browne bound her feet for several months when she was a child, a pretentious reversal of her unusual abilities as a sprinter. Now, a magazine writer with a whip hand, she wraps her divine pink toes in a silk sash once or twice a week as a form of meditation.

China, an urban tribal mixedblood, is an ardent theorist but not a methodologist. Most of her theories, however, are developed from interviews and conversations rather than from imaginative thoughts or original ideas. Her imagination is limited by narcissism but she admires, and follows from time to time, creative people. She pursued Griever de Hocus and borrowed from him one of her theories about differences in world views: Tribal children, she explained, have a passive world view because they now ride in the back of pickup trucks on the reservation and see the end of landscapes rather than what comes down the road and over the mount. "Once we were a people of the sunrise, we rode into the light," she wrote in an editorial column, "but now we watch the sunsets."

Griever remembers with pleasure the first time he watched her draw the blue sash through her small toes. She allowed him to watch but not touch, peculiar meditation and pure eroticism.

"American Indian men have little body hair," she told an audience at a conference on tribal identities, "because they ate maize which contains female hormones."

"What about corn whiskey then?" she was asked.

"The more you drink the less you need to shave," she snapped back in a firm tone of voice. "The estrogen in maize makes some men better women," she continued. "De Hocus told me that tribal tricksters are androgynous corn planters."

China first met Griever while she was eating lunch at the Swallow Restaurant outside the Pacific Film Archives in the University Museum at Berkeley. Griever had unplugged a work of art and the outcome of his art became a new part of one of her theories. "Men have no natural connections to the earth," she wrote in her journal. "Men are separated, and so they become tricksters to survive, too much trickster in a woman is a man."

Griever pulled the plug and stopped the loud whistle from a teakettle which was on a hotplate in the center of a mound of boulders and broken bricks. This mound, placed in the museum as a work of art, was covered with soiled clothing.

China looked up from her fruit salad when the shrill sound of the whistle stopped. Griever was applauded by the restaurant customers but before he could take much pleasure in his act a security guard grabbed him from behind—he had touched and interrupted a work of art. Griever resisted and threw the guard down; he wrestled with her in the middle of the work of art until the police arrived.

China, who had written about noise, cited state and federal legislation on acceptable decibel levels in public places; her presentation was so impressive that the police issued a citation to the museum for noise pollution. Griever whispered his concern about the environment. China listened and watched him finish her fruit salad. His whole face broke into words; fingers, knees, feet, and the furniture within his reach, moved when he spoke.

At the initial court hearing the museum directors argued that a work of art is not a form of pollution: "Imaginative noise indeed, but this is not the same as a cement truck or an unmuffled motorcycle." The court ruled in favor of the museum.

China wrote about the adventure for a magazine. The article appeared with photographs and a series of cartoons. In one a police officer pinched her nose, in the second cartoon the guard held her hands over her mouth, and in the last one a viewer held his hands over his ears. The morning after the article appeared, Griever rented a motorcycle, disconnected the muffler and roared through the museum around the teakettle. He was arrested and jailed. China arranged for his release on bail. Since then, she has followed him to two continents and has written several stories about his imaginative confrontations with the world.

China connects time, place, and common events to weather conditions and her various theories. For example, last month she ordered copies of "The Mystic Warrior," a television film, to preview but the video tape disintegrated in the recorder. An engineer told her that the tapes appeared to have generated their own intense heat and fused to the machine. He seemed to apologize for his mythic explanation, "'The Mystic Warriors' committed a video suicide." She never thought too much about the mythic or technical problems until the second copies she ordered for review were struck by lightning and burned. Then, when the film ran on television, a thunder storm rattled the windows in her apartment and scrambled the romantic tribal faces on screen. She drew a sash through her nervous toes and completed her review on time.

China does not leave her stories alone with an editor. She is paternal about her ideas and images and must be present when her stories are edited for publication. Mythic tropisms in her conversations, she believes, influence editorial responses to her stories. Her editors accommodate her common insecurities.

"What are the 'mythic tropisms' this time?" the editor asked as he counted the pages of her review of "The Mystic Warrior."

"What does that mean?"

"Mythic entertainment," he responded.

Los Angeles Times Calendar Magazine:

THE MYSTIC WARRIOR
Reviewed by China Browne

Institutions are appropriate structures for the continuation of a tradition, but they are not appropriate forms for the creation of the new or the revitalization of the old.—William Irwin Thompson, *Evil and World Order,* 1976.

Ahbleza, the Mystic Warrior and precious hero in this buckskin melodrama, a five-hour ABC "Novel for Television," comes to the screen from the disputed novel *Hanta Yo* by Ruth Beebe Hill. "If it is not of the spirit," Chunksa Yuha writes in the mawkish introduction to the book about an arcane band of mystic warriors, "it is not Indian." The film, alas, like the novel, is not about real tribal people or their cultures.

"I'm working on a film script," said China.

"Really," responded the editor who can read and talk but not smile at the same time. "Mawkish introduction, no less. . . ."

Ahbleza, the dubious tribal redeemer on a white horse in this ten million dollar television film, is a white variation of the old dualities of savagism and civilization, where the savage is wild and static, noble or demonic. This theme denies the diversities of tribal imagination: nonetheless, the film reaches an eager and familiar audience.

The pretentious dialogue is humorless, and the peculiar tribal dialect, such as, "Leaders listen and now they search for truth," and, "Thirty and two of our young men killed," is stupid. These racial and cultural distortions reveal the vagaries of creators and their audiences. There is some humor in this, tribal people are famous for their crosstalks with the white world, but what drowns the potential wit of the filmic characters is the parochial need to appear authentic. As fiction, the book and the film could be romantic satires.

"Remember that story I did a few months ago on that mixed-blood trickster Griever de Hocus?" asked China.

"Yes, the noise freak," said the editor.

"Well, Griever has a luminous hand . . ."

"What?" he asked and continued editing the review.

"His hand, it glows . . ."

"Jesus."

"My script is about that, about bioluminescence."

"Freak of the fireflies."

Ahbleza has a wild vision, enhanced by an untribal chorale, and then he matures on the screen like a mouth warrior—too much abstruse talk around tepee fires in the summer. A woman dressed in designer leathers chooses the hero as her lover: meanwhile, he resists violence and spooks his savage tribal enemies with an eclipse of the sun. Later, his pregnant lover leaps from a precipice to avoid tribal avengers. The hero and his warriors lose their center and hit the trail to the nearest men with "hairy faces," their first encounter with white peddlers on the prairie. Innocent tribal women discover calico cloth and their visage in hand mirrors; the errant warriors are debauched with alcohol, or "firewater," and dance drunk in the dark with their new rifles, or "firesticks."

"When he touches the thigh on a wooden statue at King's College Chapel his hand becomes luminous," said China.

"The human light bulb?" mocked the editor.

Ahbleza, the sober and virtuous hero, comes close to allegories at the end of the film: He rides his white horse to the top of a high hill where he is surrounded by savage marauders with wild face paint.

"I am a peace man," said the hero to his enemies, but no one listened. He was shot in the heart, through the sacred peace shirt that he had inherited from a traditional elder who told him: "Honor goes to the man who kills, greater honor to the man who heals." Our hero on the white horse was neither a killer nor healer, he was a victim. This romantic fatalism is a myopic theme in histories and films about tribal cultures.

The Mystic Warrior, in the end, becomes the common victim of culture contacts, technologies, and turns in civilization, because white audiences better understand that simple message. The tribal hero could never be like Jesus Christ, though he is accompanied on screen with choral music befitting a monotheistic creator. Ahbleza is not transformed, nor is he a redeemer in the real world. He remains a romantic savage resurrected in racist themes to ease a white audience through their mythic fears in the dark.

"Luminous Griever could be as hot as the Shroud of Turin," China said as she leaned over the editor when he made a mark on her story.

"Our resident metapragmatists," said the editor. He shook his head, sharpened his pencil, and continued editing the story. "Spare me the details."

"Right."

"This film violates everything I know about tribal cultures," said Terry Wilson, associate professor of Native American history at the University of California, Berkeley. "The concept of peace, for example, connotes simplistic goodness and forces the warrior societies into a position of being evil.

"Warrior societies were a way of life, not a simple form of revenge. A warrior is a state of being, a ritual act of survival, not the structural opposite of peace or goodness," Wilson said in an interview. "The tribal world is more complex than dichotomies of good and evil."

"Listen to this." China opened her notebook.

"Dichotomies of good and evil?"

"Right."

"Who can tell the difference?"

"Indians."

"Teachers and preachers too, no doubt."

"Right, listen to this."

"How can I resist," said the editor as he turned to the next page of her review. He scratched his head with a pencil.

"Court Circular, Buckingham Palace. . . ."

"Royalty in the first paragraph?"

"Griever de Hocus was received in audience by The Queen this morning and kissed her luminous hand. . . ." She continued to read from her notebook.

Richard Heffron, director of "The Mystic Warrior," explained that the characters and events in his film are "fiction but not inconceivable." Novelist Hill protested that *Hanta Yo* was not a work of fiction. The surreal scenes in the novel and the film could be viewed as authentic to an audience unfamiliar with tribal people and cultures.

Promotional material on the film announces that tribal cultures are "almost all but forgotten. Today, there are few who remember the ancient songs and ceremonies of these deeply religious people who respected the earth, regarding nothing more sacred than the right of choice. . . . Theirs was an old and spiritual way of life that was to end, abruptly and tragically, with the coming of the white man. . . ." Here again, tribal cultures are viewed as romantic victims of civilization.

"This picture is for a secular audience," the director insisted, but at the same time the film is promoted as an observance of the sacred. Heffron said that it would be much more difficult to make a dramatic film about tribal people for a tribal audience because traditional tribal people never "have eye contact, they never touch, and do not carry on conversations" like white people. He said he avoided the subtle sounds of tribal music in this film because the beat of the drum and the tones of the flute would not suggest to the audience the "emotional impact and sense of myth and grandeur" in a traditional tribal world. How ironic, it seems, that a white audience would better understand a tribal vision with the harmonic voices of a chorale. Heffron has also directed "I Will

Fight No More Forever," the television film about Chief Joseph and the Nez Perce Indians.

David Wolper, producer of "Roots: The Next Generation," and "The Thorn Birds," and now "The Mystic Warrior," claims that the novel *Hanta Yo* is "a masterpiece. This epic book makes every other book about Indians seem shallow and out of date." Such hyperbole produces income in the entertainment business, but not at the expense of published authors such as N. Scott Momaday, Leslie Silko, Paula Gunn Allen, Louise Erdrich, David Edmunds, and Vine Deloria, to name but a few distinguished writers from various tribal cultures. One word from any one of these writers would have made his "red roots" investment a better film.

"Griever de Hocus was received in audience by The Queen this morning and kissed her luminous hand on his appointment as British High Commissioner to the Council on Bioluminescence."

"De Hocus deserves you," mumbled the editor.

"The Torcher and his wife Lettice Swann had the honour of being received by Her Majesty," China continued to read from her notebook.

"Jesus. . . ."

Hanta Yo was published more than five years ago and since then the book has been the cause of more rancor in tribal circles than the rumored resurrection of General George Custer. Critics have exposed and measured the ostentatious claims the author and her trusted advisor have made about the authenticities of characters, events, and tribal behavior.

"I am Chunksa Yuha," the advisor writes in the introduction to the novel, "one of eight Dakotah boys to whom the old, old men of the tribe taught the suppressed songs and ceremonies, material suppressed for two hundred years, suppressed until now, until this book *Hanta Yo*."

Hill wrote that the "American Indian, even before Columbus, was the remnant of a very old race in its final stage, a race that had attained perhaps the highest working concept of individualism ever practiced. . . . His was the spirit not seeking truth but holding on to truth. . . . This book abounds in rhetorical questions. But the rhetorical was the only form of questioning the Indian stopused; he never answered to anyone but himself. He conjugates the verb 'think' in the first person singular only; he never presumes." Hill writes about people from her imagination, perhaps the tribes she would like to live with rather than the cultures she has studied. She is not the first person to homogenize tribal cultures under the generic name Indian, but her nominal metahistories precede written languages and the explorers and social scientists who misnamed the tribes.

"Her Majesty wore green sunglasses," said China.

"Griever, the world according to Griever," the editor exclaimed, "what is it with you and this character."

"Words and images."

"Words?"

"Griever unpeels words like oranges," said China.

"Jesus."

"Griever Christ, he delivers myths."

"Griever and David Wolper," the editor concluded.

Robert Berkhofer writes in *The White Man's Indian* that the "idea and the image of the Indian must be a White conception. Native Americans were and are real, but the Indian was a White invention and still remains largely a White image, if not stereotype . . . The first residents of the Americas were by modern estimates divided into at least two thousand cultures and more societies, practiced a multiplicity of customs and lifestyles, held an enormous variety of values and beliefs, spoke numerous languages mutually unintelligible to the many speakers, and did not conceive of themselves as a single people. . . ."

Hill has also invented an arcane language which she claims was first translated into a tribal tongue and then twisted back again. This peculiar method, she explained, produced an authentic language. The nighthawk, for example, becomes "Bird who comes at dusk and splashes in the air," in her final translation.

Allen Taylor, professor of linguistics at the University of Colorado, Boulder, writes that *Hanta Yo* "is offensive to an intelligent and literate reader because its purple prose is unable to either inform or entertain. . . . It is merely the latest of a long line of potboilers which take an Indian theme and use it to present a

European viewpoint." Taylor questions the translations of the book and concludes that "Even if one were to grant that it is possible to translate a work into an extinct, unwritten dialect, there is no reason why it should be translated back into another extinct dialect. . . .

"In my opinion, the book is a classic of poor writing. It is repetitious and overly long, and it distorts and trivializes what it attempts to present sympathetically. It is a propagandistic work which perpetuates pre-scientific, romantic myths about language, culture, and American Indians which are better forgotten."

The producers, director, and the author, appear to be enrolled in a new order of cultural missionaries. First there were anthropologists, now there are television movies to deliver the myths of the tribal past.

Remember, you agreed with me on the lift: If you can hire Mormon Indians to dance at dusk on the ski slopes and name your lift after the Mandan then you can finance a feature film about mixedbloods. Hope to hear from you soon.

Peace on you,
Griever

Griever de Hocus
Trinity House
Savage Gardens, London

Dear Griever:
  Your script proposal is a rich slice of mixedblood tribal kitsch. We should talk more about your luminous ideas. Keep your hand in the fire. The Mandan ride was unforgettable.
Best Wishes,

Ordinary Bob

THE END

SIMON ORTIZ

Simon Ortiz was born in Albuquerque in 1941 and raised in the Acoma pueblo community in western New Mexico. The Acomas are closely related to the Lagunas. Many Americans imagine reservations, especially in the desert southwest, to be dreary, ugly places; but Acoma, or Sky City, as it is called locally, is spectacularly beautiful. Originally situated to protect the tribe against attacks from the plains tribes and the Spanish, Acoma sits atop a high mesa with very steep walls.

Ortiz attended the Universities of New Mexico and Iowa and has taught Indian literature and creative writing at San Diego State, Navajo Community College (Tsaile, Arizona), and the University of New Mexico.

Known primarily for his poetry, Ortiz published his fist book of verse, *Going for the Rain,* in 1976. The collection features a number of poems about Coyote, Ortiz's trickster. To date Ortiz has published four books of poetry.

Ortiz is an accomplished fiction writer as well, have also published two collections of short stories. The first, *Howbah Indians,* appeared in 1978. The two selections in this anthology are from *Fightin',* published in 1983.

The first of our stories, "Crossing," concerns middle-class Indians, a brother and sister who have been living in the San Francisco Bay Area. She is finishing her degree at Stanford Law School; we never find out exactly what he has been doing. The pair contrast their lives in the American mainstream with the misery of their forebears who were forced by poverty to leave their tribal lands in New Mexico to work under deplorable conditions for the railroad in California.

The second story, "Men on the Moon," is a tour de force. It is an account of the 1969 moon landing told from the point of view of an old Indian man who is watching the event on television even though he understands very little of the "Mericano" language. Through the old man's naivete and confusion, Ortiz questions the wisdom of the people who undertake moon shots in their quest for knowledge while ignoring much of what they should know about life on earth.

After five years in California, Charley Colorado was on his way back home to New Mexico. He had stopped to visit with his sister, Dianne, who lived in Palo Alto.

"Five years," he said, "I don't know what I expected but I don't have much to show for having come to California."

It was late afternoon, and they had been talking for a long time in Dianne's apartment. It was different now—that much was certain. Dianne was finishing law school and he had worked in San Francisco for five years. Indians were places they had never been; they were doing things they hadn't done before. They had talked about that, had even agreed on the certainty, and now they had grown quiet.

After a while, Charley picked up a photograph from a TV stand. He turned it over and read, Charles and Dianne 1961.

"I didn't know you had this. Do you remember where the photograph was taken?" Charley asked.

"It was in southern California where Dad was working. Mama, you and I went to visit him that summer. You were in your first year of Indian School," Dianne said.

"We went by train," Charley said. "Dad met us in Barstow and we stayed with relatives at the Indian Colony. Next day, we went where the track gang was, near San Clemente. You and I wanted to see the ocean right away, and we all walked down to the beach. I was so excited and scared when the ocean came into view. It took my breath away."

"You look so serious in the picture, Charley," Dianne said. "Just like you look now." She laughed.

Charley laughed too. "I was scared. I didn't like where Dad lived, that box bunk car. The whole thing would shake whenever a train passed by on the next track."

"We didn't stay there long," Dianne said. "We went back to the Indian Colony. Such a name, but that's what it was. The railroad company brought Indian people from New Mexico and put them in little firetrap houses on company owned land by the railroad yards."

The brother and sister both knew very certainly what had happened. After the railroad had taken the very best lands along the river in the 1890s, Indians couldn't make a living from the land they had left. So they took jobs on the railroad in meager compensation.

"Daddy would come home from laying track, and he would be all grimy and exhausted, groaning from pained muscles. It's no wonder he and other men drank until they couldn't feel anything."

Charley would be dismayed. His father's speech would slur and he would stumble around when he was usually so graceful. Drunkenness was common at the Colony; there were always fights, there was always screaming. He would hide every time his father and the other men got drunk. At the Indian Colony, he would see the men trudging off to work in the mornings and returning in the evenings looking like they had just lost a battle.

"Do you remember that story Grandpa Santiago would tell? It was after the railroad came. Things had become so poor, the people were sick, there wasn't much to eat. There was little useful land left. The men decided to leave the Pueblo to find work." Dianne was simply stating a fact and a remembrance told by their grandfather when they were children.

"He said, 'The men packed provisions for a long journey on burros and horses. Some men had neither so they were to take turns riding and walking. I was this tall, just a small boy. There was a great flurry of activity and apprehension for who knew what might happen—there were unforeseen events and even danger. But being very young, I found it of great excitement. There was weeping upon the leave-taking. Wives, mothers, sons, daughters, beloved ones were crying and calling to them—Be well, avoid danger, come back; may fortune and the guiding spirits of our people be with you. They left singing this song:

Kalrrahuurrniah ah
Kalrrahuurrniah ah
Steh ehyuu uuh.

From the edge of the Pueblo, our homeland, we watched them until they disappeared into the west.'"

Yes, Charley remembered clearly the old man speaking; his voice had been somewhat sad but always resolute, knowing what had happened. 'There was an old old woman who could not see very well, who kept looking to the west long long after the men had left. She kept murmuring prayers and saying, Tell the rain to come, young men. When you meet the clouds at the western edge, tell them we need their help. Bring the rain home with you, young men, from that great water. Your journey will be for all of us, young men, and for the land. And she sang. My brother and I sat with the old woman until it was too dark to see anything but the faint light over the mountains and a few red clouds. I imagined it was dust clouds being raised by the burros and men.'

"Those men from the Pueblo decided to do what was necessary," Dianne said. "There was nothing else they could do; they had to try. It may sound odd, but they were like the Okies who, later on, came to California. What land they had left was worthless. No living could be made off it; the Okies couldn't either. It wasn't only the duststorms, like some historians would have us believe. The people were being forced off the land."

Charley had asked his mother for details of the journey taken by the men. She told him, It happened that they arrived at a big river after they had travelled for many days. At the river, they were stopped by men who demanded payment for crossing the river which was a border. The men had guns and they told our beloved men they could cross only if they made payment for passage on a boat.

The men didn't have any money. All they had was the desire to work; that's why they had made the decision to go to California. So they didn't know what to do at first. Some wanted to cross at another place but others said it would be dangerous. There were men with guns on the other side of the river who would demand paper evidence of having paid for crossing. Some men said it was fruitless to go on and they wanted to go home.

We all have to be of one mind and purpose and we all have to decide, the leaders said. We came on this journey to find work because we have the ability and the desire to work, but it is obvious these people here will not let us pass without payment and they have said they do not want more Indians in their state anyway. But we have a purpose, to help our people who are suffering a difficult time—remember them. So the men, beloved, decided to sell what possessions they had, their burros and horses and even their weapons, in order to pay for the passage of several of their number.

It must have been a sad time, Charley's mother said. When the men who couldn't cross returned home, they almost had nothing left. It was about 1911, and it was a dim and hard time for our people then.

Dianne said to Charley, "For a long time, I thought the story was kind of sad because most of the men didn't get to California and they returned with nothing. But then, thinking about it, it's not sad. The men decided what to do. They sold everything in order to have a few go on. They didn't just turn back. A few would make that crossing for whatever it meant—to make a living, to summon the rain from the ocean—just as they had all set out to do. I only heard Santiago tell the story when we were children but I remember every detail."

The next morning came with the sunlight streaming through thin curtains unto the red carpet of Dianne's apartment. For several moments, Charley, lying face down on the edge of the sofa bed made up for him by his sister, could not shake the dream that was happening. First One was shouting, Come, hurry, we're almost there!

He could barely hear the shout as it came from a vast distance across a valley. And the valley was filled with a furious molten motion of lava which hissed, and sputtered, and leaped up in rippling surges.

He, the Second One, was afraid and he trembled. First One called again. Even at the distance, Second One could see that where his brother was it was green, lush with grass, and the land above and beyond him was filled with tall trees. And above the trees and beyond were clouds, white and thick rain clouds.

They had been sent to take word to the rain clouds. But his fear froze him to the ground, and he could not move. The very ground, rocky and barren, he stood upon shook with the surging of the molten rock. He was desperate; he did not want to fail; the people were waiting for the rain.

Faintly, across the vast fearsome valley, he heard his brother's voice call, "Look behind you!"

He looked and there was nothing but barren rocky hills and dried tree trunks and beyond that the flat white sky. What was he to see? he moaned with a parched throat. And then in the distance, indistinct at first, coming very slowly, was someone. His eyes burning, he strained to see who it was.

It was an old woman with white hair, painfully making her way among huge boulders in her way, and she was blind. Without thinking, Second One ran to her and said, Grandmother, there is danger ahead, you should not be walking towards it; turn back. And the old woman looked at him with her white-turned eyes and said, Grandson, I have come to help you on your mission to help the people and the land.

She was so old even her words were slow, and she put her hand in an apron pocket and brought out a flowered handkerchief. Untying the knot, she showed him a white stone nestled in corn-meal, and she drew the stone out and handed it to him.

Take this, she said, tie it to your arrow and let it fly across to the other side. She took the cornmeal and breathing upon it all around in a circle to the horizons, she sprinkled it on the ground and shook out her handkerchief.

He did as he was told, quickly tied the stone to the arrow-shaft with sinew, and then pulling on his bow with all his might, he let the arrow fly. It flew until he lost sight of it and suddenly in the path of its flight appeared a silver thread arcing above the ferocious valley of lava.

Quickly, Grandson, the old woman said, go as fast as you can. Don't worry, it will hold you.

Calling, "Thank you, Grandmother," he stepped on the thread and ran as fast as he could. From below, he could feel the furious red heat leaping up to his face.

Charley shook his head and squinted his eyes at the morning light falling on his face and the carpet. "Thank you," he said quietly. "All around and beyond, thank you, for the journey here and for the journey home to the Pueblo and for the crossing, thank you."

Men on the Moon

Joselita brought her father, Faustin, the TV on Father's Day. She brought it over after Sunday mass and she had her son hook up the antenna. She plugged the TV into the wall socket.

Faustin sat on a worn couch. He was covered with an old coat. He had worn that coat for twenty years.

It's ready. Turn it on and I'll adjust the antenna, Amarosho told his mother. The TV warmed up and then it flickered into dull light. It was snowing. Amarosho tuned it a bit. It snowed less and then a picture formed.

Look, Naishtiya, Joselita said. She touched her father's hand and pointed at the TV.

I'll turn the antenna a bit and you tell me when the picture is clear, Amarosho said. He climbed on the roof again.

After a while the picture turned clearer. It's better, his mother shouted. There was only the tiniest bit of snow falling.

That's about the best it can get I guess, Amarosho said. Maybe it'll clear up on the other channels. He turned the selector. It was clearer on another.

There were two men struggling with each other. Wrestling, Amarosho said. Do you want to watch wrestling? Two men are fighting, Nana. One of them is Apache Red. Chiseh tsah, he told his grandfather.

The old man stirred. He had been staring intently into the TV. He wondered why there was so much snow at first. Now there were two men fighting. One of them was Chiseh, an Apache, and the other was a Mericano. There were people shouting excitedly and clapping hands within the TV.

The two men backed away from each other once in a while and then they clenched. They wheeled mightily and suddenly one threw the other. The old man smiled. He wondered why they were fighting.

Something else showed on the TV screen. A bottle of wine was being poured. The old man liked the pouring sound and he moved his mouth. Someone was selling wine.

The two fighting men came back on the TV. They struggled with each other and after a while one of them didn't get up and then another person came and held up the hand of the Apache who was dancing around in a feathered headdress.

It's over, Amarosho announced. Apache Red won the fight, Nana.

The Chiseh won. Faustin watched the other one, a light-haired man who looked totally exhausted and angry with himself. He didn't like the Apache too much. He wanted them to fight again.

After a few moments something else appeared on the TV.

What is that? Faustin asked. There was an object with smoke coming from it. It was standing upright.

Men are going to the moon, Nana, his grandson said. It's Apollo. It's going to fly three men to the moon.

That thing is going to fly to the moon?

Yes, Nana.

What is it called again?

Apollo, a spaceship rocket, Joselita told her father.

The Apollo spaceship stood on the ground emitting clouds of something that looked like smoke.

A man was talking, telling about the plans for the flight, what would happen, that it was almost time. Faustin could not understand the man very well because he didn't know many words in Mericano.

He must be talking about that thing flying in the air? he said.

Yes. It's about ready to fly away to the moon.

Faustin remembered that the evening before he had looked at the sky and seen that the moon was almost in the middle phase. He wondered if it was important that the men get to the moon.

Are those men looking for something on the moon? he asked his grandson.

They're trying to find out what's on the moon, Nana, what kind of dirt and rocks there are, to see if there's any life on the moon. The men are looking for knowledge, Amarosho told him.

Faustin wondered if the men had run out of places to look for knowledge on the earth. Do they know if they'll find knowledge? he asked.

They have some information already. They've gone before and come back. They're going again.

Did they bring any back?

They brought back some rocks.

Rocks. Faustin laughed quietly. The scientist men went to search for knowledge on the moon and they brought back rocks. He thought that perhaps Amarosho was joking with him. The grandson had gone to Indian School for a number of years and sometimes he would tell his grandfather some strange and funny things.

The old man was suspicious. They joked around a lot. Rocks— you sure that's all they brought back?

That's right, Nana, only rocks and some dirt and pictures they made of what it looks like on the moon.

The TV picture was filled with the rocket, close up now. Men were sitting and moving around by some machinery and the voice had become more urgent. The old man watched the activity in the picture intently but with a slight smile on his face.

Suddenly it became very quiet, and the voice was firm and commanding and curiously pleading. Ten, nine, eight, seven, six, five, four, three, two, liftoff. The white smoke became furious and a muted rumble shook through the TV. The rocket was trembling and the voice was trembling.

It was really happening, the old man marvelled. Somewhere inside of that cylinder with a point at its top and long slender wings were three men who were flying to the moon.

The rocket rose from the ground. There were enormous clouds of smoke and the picture shook. Even the old man became tense and he grasped the edge of the couch. The rocket spaceship rose and rose.

There's fire coming out of the rocket, Amarosho explained. That's what makes it go.

Fire. Faustin had wondered what made it fly. He'd seen pictures of other flying machines. They had long wings and someone had explained to him that there was machinery inside which spun metal blades which made them fly. He had wondered what made this thing fly. He hoped his grandson wasn't joking him.

After a while there was nothing but the sky. The rocket Apollo had disappeared. It hadn't taken very long and the voice from the TV wasn't excited anymore. In fact the voice was very calm and almost bored.

I have to go now, Naishtiya, Joselita told her father. I have things to do.

Me, too, Amarosho said.

Wait, the old man said, wait. What shall I do with this thing. What is it you call it?

TV, his daughter said. You watch it. You turn it on and you watch it.

I mean how do you stop it. Does it stop like the radio, like the mahkina? It stops?

This way, Nana, Amarosho said and showed his grandfather. He turned the dial and the picture went away. He turned the dial again and the picture flickered on again. Were you afraid this one-eye would be looking at you all the time? Amarosho laughed and gently patted the old man's shoulder.

Faustin was relieved. Joselita and her son left. He watched the TV for a while. A lot of activity was going on, a lot of men were moving among machinery, and a couple of men were talking. And then it showed the rocket again.

He watched it rise and fly away again. It disappeared again. There was nothing but the sky. He turned the dial and the picture died away. He turned it on and the picture came on again. He turned it off. He went outside and to a fence a distance from his home. When he finished he studied the sky for a while.

II

That night, he dreamed.

Flintwing Boy was watching a Skquuyuh mahkina come down a hill. The mahkina made a humming noise. It was walking. It shone in the sunlight. Flintwing Boy moved to a better position to see. The mahkina kept on moving. It was moving towards him.

The Skquuyuh mahkina drew closer. Its metal legs stepped upon trees and crushed growing flowers and grass. A deer bounded away frightened. Tshushki came running to Flintwing Boy.

Anaweh, he cried, trying to catch his breath.

The coyote was staring at the thing which was coming towards them. There was wild fear in his eyes.

What is that, Anaweh? What is that thing? he gasped.

It looks like a mahkina, but I've never seen one like it before. It must be some kind of Skquuyuh mahkina.

Where did it come from?

I'm not sure yet, Anaweh, Flintwing Boy said. When he saw that Tshushki was trembling with fear, he said gently, Sit down, Anaweh. Rest yourself. We'll find out soon enough.

The Skquuyuh mahkina was undeterred. It walked over and through everything. It splashed through a stream of clear water. The water boiled and streaks of oil flowed downstream. It split a juniper tree in half with a terrible crash. It crushed a boulder into dust with a sound of heavy metal. Nothing stopped the Skquuyuh mahkina. It hummed.

Anaweh, Tshushki cried, what shall we do? What can we do?

Flintwing Boy reached into the bag at his side. He took out an object. It was a flint arrowhead. He took out some cornfood.

Come over here, Anaweh. Come over here. Be calm, he motioned to the frightened coyote. He touched the coyote in several places of his body with the arrowhead and put cornfood in the palm of his hand.

This way, Flintwing Boy said and closed Tshushki's fingers over the cornfood gently. And they faced east. Flintwing Boy said, We humble ourselves again. We look in your direction for guidance. We ask for your protection. We humble our poor bodies and spirits because only you are the power and the source and the knowledge. Help us then—that is all we ask.

They breathed on the cornfood and took in the breath of all directions and gave the cornfood unto the ground.

Now the ground trembled with the awesome power of the

Skquuyuh mahkina. Its humming vibrated against everything. Flintwing Boy reached behind him and took several arrows from his quiver. He inspected them carefully and without any rush he fit one to his bowstring.

And now, Anaweh, you must go and tell everyone. Describe what you have seen. The people must talk among themselves and decide what it is about and what they will do. You must hurry but you must not alarm the people. Tell them I am here to meet it. I will give them my report when I find out.

Coyote turned and began to run. He stopped several yards away. Hahtrudzaimeh, he called. Like a man of courage, Anaweh, like a man.

The old man stirred in his sleep. A dog was barking. He awoke and got out of his bed and went outside. The moon was past the midpoint and it would be morning light in a few hours.

III

Later, the spaceship reached the moon.

Amarosho was with his grandfather. They watched a replay of two men walking on the moon.

So that's the men on the moon, Faustin said.

Yes, Nana, that's it.

There were two men inside of heavy clothing and equipment. The TV picture showed a closeup of one of them and indeed there was a man's face inside of glass. The face moved its mouth and smiled and spoke but the voice seemed to be separate from the face.

It must be cold. They have heavy clothing on, Faustin said.

It's supposed to be very cold and very hot. They wear the clothes and other things for protection from the cold and heat, Amarosho said.

The men on the moon were moving slowly. One of them skipped and he floated alongside the other.

The old man wondered if they were underwater. They seem to be able to float, he said.

The information I have heard is that a man weighs less than he does on earth, much less, and he floats. There is no air easier to breathe. Those boxes on their backs contain air for them to breathe, Amarosho told his grandfather.

He weighs less, the old man wondered, and there is no air except for the boxes on their backs. He looked at Amarosho but his grandson didn't seem to be joking with him.

The land on the moon looked very dry. It looked like it had not rained for a long, long time. There were no trees, no plants, no grass. Nothing but dirt and rocks, a desert.

Amarosho had told him that men on earth—the scientists— believed there was no life on the moon. Yet those men were trying to find knowledge on the moon. He wondered if perhaps they had special tools with which they could find knowledge even if they believed there was no life on the moon desert.

The mahkina sat on the desert. It didn't make a sound. Its metal feet were planted flat on the ground. It looked somewhat awkward. Faustin searched vainly around the mahkina but there didn't seem to be anything except the dry land on the TV. He couldn't figure out the mahkina. He wasn't sure whether it could move and could cause fear. He didn't want to ask his grandson that question.

After a while, one of the bulky men was digging in the ground. He carried a long thin hoe with which he scooped dirt and put it into a container. He did this for a while.

Is he going to bring the dirt back to earth too? Faustin asked.

I think he is, Nana, Amarosho said. Maybe he'll get some rocks too. Watch.

Indeed several minutes later the man lumbered over to a pile of rocks and gathered several handsize ones. He held them out proudly. They looked just like rocks from around anyplace. The voice from the TV seemed to be excited about the rocks.

They will study the rocks too for knowledge?

Yes, Nana.

What will they use the knowledge for, Nana?

They say they will use it to better mankind, Nana. I've heard that. And to learn more about the universe we live in. Also some of them say that the knowledge will be useful in finding out where everything began and how everything was made.

Faustin smiled at his grandson. He said, You are telling me the true facts aren't you?

Why yes, Nana. That's what they say. I'm not just making it up, Amarosho said.

Well then—do they say why they need to know where everything began? Hasn't anyone ever told them?

I think other people have tried to tell them but they want to find out for themselves and also I think they claim they don't know enough and need to know more and for certain, Amarosho said.

The man in the bulky suit had a small pickaxe in his hand. He was striking at a boulder. The breathing of the man could clearly be heard. He seemed to be working very hard and was very tired.

Faustin had once watched a crew of Mericano drilling for water. They had brought a tall mahkina with a loud motor. The mahkina would raise a limb at its center to its very top and then drop it with a heavy and loud metal clang. The mahkina and its men sat at one spot for several days and finally they found water.

The water had bubbled out weakly, gray-looking and didn't look drinkable at all. And then they lowered the mahkina, put their equipment away and drove away. The water stopped flowing.

After a couple of days he went and checked out the place. There was nothing there except a pile of gray dirt and an indentation in the ground. The ground was already dry and there were dark spots of oil-soaked dirt.

He decided to tell Amarosho about the dream he had.

After the old man finished, Amarosho said, Old man, you're telling me the truth now? You know that you have become somewhat of a liar. He was teasing his grandfather.

Yes, Nana. I have told you the truth as it occurred to me that night. Everything happened like that except that I might not have recalled everything about it.

That's some story, Nana, but it's a dream.

It's a dream but it's the truth, Faustin said.

I believe you, Nana, his grandson said.

LOUISE ERDRICH

Born in 1954 in Little Falls, Minnesota, Louise Erdrich was raised in Wahpeton, North Dakota. She is a member of the Turtle Mountain band of Chippewas. She received her B.A. from Dartmouth and her M.A. from Johns Hopkins.

Erdrich has published a book of poems, *Jacklight* (1984), and three novels, *Love Medicine* (1984), *The Beet Queen* (1986), and *Tracks* (1988). The novels are part of a cycle portraying the life of Chippewas (Erdrich prefers "Chippewa" to "Anishinaabe"; the tribe is the same), mixed-bloods, and whites in rural North Dakota over a period of five generations. Erdrich presents a cast of characters whose venality, grotesqueness, libidinousness, and wonderful humanity would make them fit company for Chaucer's pilgrims.

Our selection, "Love Medicine," is the title story (the chapters are sufficiently independent to stand as short stories) from Erdrich's first novel. The hero is a bumbling but lovable idiot named Lipsha Morrissey, whose malapropisms—for example, God smiting the "Phillipines"—are inspired. Religions are usually syncretic, but Lipsha's is particularly eclectic. He attempts to bring his grandmother and grandfather closer by use of Chippewa love medicine, and tries to enlist the aid of the local priest in the enterprise. The mixture of pathos and humor in the story is very effective. Great comic authors are often moving as well as funny, but only the greatest—Shakespeare and Faulkner, for instance—are both at once. It may sound hyperbolic to include Erdrich in that company, but her account of the way Lipsha and his grandmother accidentally kill Nector Kashpaw is reminiscent of Shakespeare's account of the death of Falstaff in the way it combines humor and pathos.

Lipsha Morrissey

I never really done much with my life, I suppose. I never had a television. Grandma Kashpaw had one inside her apartment at the Senior Citizens, so I used to go there and watch my favorite shows. For a while she used to call me the biggest waste on the reservation and hark back to how she saved me from my own mother, who wanted to tie me in a potato sack and throw me in a slough. Sure, I was grateful to Grandma Kashpaw for saving me like that, for raising me, but gratitude gets old. After a while, stale. I had to stop thanking her. One day I told her I had paid her back in full by staying at her beck and call. I'd do anything for Grandma. She knew that. Besides, I took care of Grandpa like nobody else could, on account of what a handful he'd gotten to be.

But that was nothing. I know the tricks of mind and body inside out without ever having trained for it, because I got the touch. It's a thing you got to be born with. I got secrets in my hands that nobody ever knew to ask. Take Grandma Kashpaw with her tired veins all knotted up in her legs like clumps of blue snails. I take my fingers and I snap them on the knots. The medicine flows out of me. The touch. I run my fingers up the maps of those rivers of veins or I knock very gentle above their hearts or I make a circling motion on their stomachs, and it helps them. They feel much better. Some women pay me five dollars.

I couldn't do the touch for Grandpa, though. He was a hard nut. You know, some people fall right through the hole in their lives. It's invisible, but they come to it after time, never knowing where. There is this woman here, Lulu Lamartine, who always had a thing for Grandpa. She loved him since she was a girl and always said he was a genius. Now she says that his mind got so full it exploded.

How can I doubt that? I know the feeling when your mental power builds up too far. I always used to say that's why the Indians got drunk. Even statistically we're the smartest people on the earth. Anyhow with Grandpa I couldn't hardly believe it, because all my youth he stood out as a hero to me. When he started getting toward second childhood he went through different moods. He would stand in the woods and cry at the top of his shirt. It scared me, scared everyone, Grandma worst of all.

Yet he was so smart—do you believe it?—that he *knew* he was getting foolish.

He said so. He told me that December I failed school and come back on the train to Hoopdance. I didn't have nowhere else to go. He picked me up there and he said it straight out: "I'm getting into my second childhood." And then he said something else I still remember: "I been chosen for it. I couldn't say no." So I figure that a man so smart all his life—tribal chairman and the star of movies and even pictured in the statehouse and on cans of snuff—would know what he's doing by saying yes. I think he was called to second childhood like anybody else gets a call for the priesthood or the army or whatever. So I really did not listen too hard when the doctor said this was some kind of disease old people got eating too much sugar. You just can't tell me that a man who went to Washington and gave them bureaucrats what for could lose his mind from eating too much Milky Way. No, he put second childhood on himself.

Behind those songs he sings out in the middle of Mass, and back of those stories that everybody knows by heart, Grandpa is thinking hard about life. I know the feeling. Sometimes I'll throw up a smokescreen to think behind. I'll hitch up to Winnipeg and play the Space Invaders for six hours, but all the time there and back I will be thinking some fairly deep thoughts that surprise even me, and I'm used to it. As for him, if it was just the thoughts there wouldn't be no problem. Smokescreen is what irritates the social structure, see, and Grandpa has done things that just distract people to the point they want to throw him in the cookie jar where they keep the mentally insane. He's far from that, I know for sure, but even Grandma had trouble keeping her patience once he started sneaking off to Lamartine's place. He's not supposed to have his candy, and Lulu feeds it to him. That's *one* of the reasons why he goes.

Grandma tried to get me to put the touch on Grandpa soon after he began stepping out. I didn't want to, but before Grandma started telling me again what a bad state my bare behind was in when she first took me home, I thought I should at least pretend.

I put my hands on either side of Grandpa's head. You wouldn't look at him and say he was crazy. He's a fine figure of a man, as Lamartine would say, with all his hair and half his teeth, a beak like a hawk, and cheeks like the blades of a hatchet. They put his picture on all the tourist guides to North Dakota and even copied his face for artistic paintings. I guess you could call him a monument all of himself. He started grinning when I put my hands on his templates, and I knew right then he knew how come I touched him. I knew the smokescreen was going to fall.

And I was right: just for a moment it fell.

"Let's pitch whoopee," he said across my shoulder Grandma.

They don't use that expression much around here anymore, but for damn sure it must have meant something. It got her goat right quick.

She threw my hands off his head herself and stood in front of him, overmatching him pound for pound, and taller too, for she had a growth spurt in middle age while he had shrunk, so now the length and breadth of her surpassed him. She glared up and spoke her piece into his face about how he was off at all hours tomcatting and chasing Lamartine again and making a damn old fool of himself.

"And you got no more whoopee to pitch anymore anyhow!" she yelled at last, surprising me so my jaw just dropped, for us kids all had pretended for so long that those rustling sounds we heard from their side of the room at night never happened. She sure had pretended it, up till now, anyway. I saw that tears were in her eyes. And that's when I saw how much grief and love she felt for him. And it gave me a real shock to the system. You see I thought love got easier over the years so it didn't hurt so bad when it hurt, or feel so good when it felt good. I thought it smoothed out and old people hardly noticed it. I thought it curled up and died, I guess. Now I saw it rear up like a whip and lash.

She loved him. She was jealous. She mourned him like the dead. And he just smiled into the air, trapped in the seams of his mind.

So I didn't know what to do. I was in a laundry then. They was like parents to me, the way they had took me home and reared me. I could see her point for wanting to get him back the way he was so at least she could argue with him, sleep with him, not be shamed out by Lamartine. She'd always love him. That hit me like a ton of bricks. For one whole day I felt this odd feeling that cramped my hands. When you have the touch, that's where longing gets you. I never loved like that. It made me feel all inspired to see them fight, and I wanted to go out and find a woman who I would love until one of us died or went crazy. But I'm not like that really. From time to time I heal a person all up good inside, however when it comes to the long shot I doubt that I got staying power.

And you need that, staying power, going out to love somebody. I knew this quality was not going to jump on me with no effort. So I turned my thoughts back to Grandma and Grandpa. I felt her side of it with my hands and my tangled guts, and I felt his side of it within the stretch of my mentality. He had gone out to lunch one day and never came back. He was fishing in the middle of Lake Turcot. And there was big thoughts on his line, and he kept throwing them back for even bigger ones that would explain to him, say, the meaning of how we got here and why we have to leave so soon. All in all, I could not see myself treating Grandpa with the touch, brining him back, when the real part of him had chose to be off thinking somewhere. It was only the rest of him that stayed around causing trouble, after all, and we could handle most of it without any problem.

Besides, it was hard to argue with his reasons for doing some things. Take Holy Mass. I used to go there just every so often, when I got frustrated mostly, because even though I know the Higher Power dwells everyplace, there's something very calming about the cool greenish inside of our mission. Or so I thought, anyway. Grandpa was the one who stripped off my delusions in this matter, for it was he who busted right through what Father Upsala calls the sacred serenity of the place.

We filed in that time. Me and Grandpa. We sat down in our pews. Then the rosary got started up pre-Mass and that's when Grandpa filled up his chest and opened his mouth and belted out them words.

HAIL MARIE FULL OF GRACE.

He had a powerful set of lungs.

And he kept on like that. He did not let up. He hollered and he yelled them prayers, and I guess people was used to him by now, because they only muttered theirs and did not quit and gawk like I did. I was getting red-faced, I admit. I give him the elbow once or twice, but that wasn't nothing to him. He kept on. He shrieked to heaven and he pleaded like a movie actor and he pounded his chest like Tarzan in the Lord I Am Not Worthies. I thought he might hurt himself. Then after a while I guess I got used to it, and that's when I wondered: how come?

So afterwards I out and asked him. "How come? How come you yelled?"

"God don't hear me otherwise," said Grandpa Kashpaw.

I sweat. I broke right into a little cold sweat at my hairline because I knew this was perfectly right and for years not one damn other person had noticed it. God's been going deaf. Since the Old Testament, God's been deafening up on us. I read, see. Besides the dictionary, which I'm constantly in use of, I had this Bible once. I read it. I found there was discrepancies between then and now. It struck me. Here God used to raineth bread from clouds, smite the Phillipines, sling fire down on red-light districts where people got stabbed. He even appeared in person every once in a while. God used to pay attention, is what I'm saying.

Now there's your God in the Old Testament and there is Chippewa Gods as well. Indian Gods, good and bad, like tricky Nanabozho or the water monster, Missepeshu, who lives over in Lake Turcot. That water monster was the last God I ever heard to appear. It had a weakness for young girls and grabbed one of the Blues off her rowboat. She got to shore all right, but only after this monster had its way with her. She's an old lady now. Old Lady Blue. She still won't let her family fish that lake.

Our Gods aren't perfect, is what I'm saying, but at least they come around. They'll do a favor if you ask them right. You don't have to yell. But you do have to know, like I said, how to ask in the right way. That makes problems, because to ask proper was an art that was lost to the Chippewas once the Catholics gained ground. Even now, I have to wonder if Higher Power turned it back, if we got to yell, or if we just don't speak its language.

I looked around me. How else could I explain what all I had seen in my short life—King smashing his fist in things, Gordie drinking himself down to the Bismarck hospitals, or Aunt June left by a white man to wander off in the snow. How else to explain the times my touch don't work, and farther back, to the old-time Indians who was swept away in the outright germ warfare and dirty-dog killing of the whites. In those times, us Indians was so much kindlier than now.

We took them in.

Oh yes, I'm bitter as an old cutworm just thinking of how they done to us and doing still.

So Grandpa Kashpaw just opened my eyes a little there. Was there any sense relying on a God whose ears was stopped? Just like the government? I says then, right off, maybe we got nothing but ourselves. And that's not much, just personally speaking. I know I don't got the cold hard potatoes it takes to understand everything. Still, there's things I'd like to do. For instance, I'd like to help some people like my Grandpa and Grandma Kashpaw get back some happiness within the tail ends of their lives.

I told you once before I couldn't see my way clear to putting the direct touch on Grandpa's mind, and I kept my moral there, but something soon happened to make me think a little bit of mental adjustment wouldn't do him and the rest of us no harm.

It was after we saw him one afternoon in the sunshine courtyard of the Senior Citizens with Lulu Lamartine. Grandpa used to like to dig there. He had his little dandelion fork out, and he was prying up them dandelions right and left while Lamartine watched him.

"He's scratching up the dirt, all right," said Grandma, watching Lamartine watch Grandpa out the window.

Now Lamartine was about half the considerable size of Grandma, but you would never think of sizes anyway. They were different in an even more noticeable way. It was the difference between a house fixed up with paint and picky fence, and a house left to weather away into the soft earth, is what I'm saying. Lamartine was jacked up, latticed, shuttered, and vinyl sided, while Grandma sagged and bulged on her slipped foundations and let her hair go the silver gray of rain-dried lumber. Right now, she eyed the Lamartine's pert flowery dress with such a look it despaired me. I knew what this could lead to with Grandma. Alternating tongue storms and rock-hard silences was hard on a man, even one who didn't notice, like Grandpa. So I went fetching him.

But he was gone when I popped through the little screen door that led out on the courtyard. There was nobody out there either, to point which way they went. Just the dandelion fork quibbling upright in the ground. That gave me an idea. I snookered over to the Lamartine's door and I listened in first, then knocked. But nobody. So I went walking through the lounges and around the card tables. Still nobody. Finally it was my touch that led me to the laundry room. I cracked the door. I went in. There they were. And he was really loving her up good, boy, and she was going hell for leather. Sheets was flapping on the lines above, and washcloths, pillowcases, shirts was also flying through the air, for they was trying to clear out a place for themselves in a high-heaped but shallow laundry cart. The washers and dryers was all on, chock full of quarters, shaking and moaning. I couldn't hear what Grandpa and the Lamartine was billing and cooing, and they couldn't hear me.

I didn't know what to do, so I went inside and shut the door.

The Lamartine wore a big curly light-brown wig. Looked like one of them squeaky little white-people dogs. Poodles they call them. Anyway, that wig is what saved us from the worse. For I could hardly shout and tell them I was in there, no more could I try and grab him. I was trapped where I was. There was nothing I could really do but hold the door shut. I was scared of somebody else upsetting in and really getting an eyeful. Turned out though, in the heat of the clinch, as I was trying to avert my eyes you see, the Lamartine's curly wig jumped off her head. And if you ever been in the midst of something and had a big change like that occur in the someone, you can't help know how it devastates your basic urges. Not only that, but her wig was almost with a life of its own. Grandpa's eyes were bugging at the change already, and swear to God if the thing didn't rear up and pop him in the face like it was going to start something. He scrambled up, Grandpa did, and the Lamartine jumped up after him all addled looking. They just stared at each other, huffing and puffing, with quizzical expression. The surprise seemed to drive all sense completely out of Grandpa's mind.

"The letter was what started the fire," he said. "I never would have done it."

"What letter?" said the Lamartine. She was stiff-necked now, and elegant, even bald, like some alien queen. I gave her back the wig. The Lamartine replaced it on her head, and whenever I saw her after that, I couldn't help thinking of her bald, with special powers, as if from another planet.

"That was a close call," I said to Grandpa after she had left.

But I think he had already forgot the incident. He just stood there all quiet and thoughtful. You really wouldn't think he was crazy. He looked like he was just about to say something important, explaining himself. He said something, all right, but it didn't have nothing to do with anything that made sense.

He wondered where the heck he put his dandelion fork. That's when I decided about the mental adjustment.

Now what was mostly our problem was not so much that he was not all there, but that what was there of him often hankered after Lamartine. If we could put a stop to that, I thought, we might be getting someplace. But here, see, my touch was of no use. For what could I snap my fingers at to make him faithful to Grandma?

Like the quality of staying power, this faithfulness was invisible. I know it's something that you got to acquire, but I never known where from. Maybe there's no rhyme or reason to it, like my getting the touch, and then again maybe it's a kind of magic.

It was Grandma Kashpaw who thought of it in the end. She knows things. Although she will not admit she has a scrap of Indian blood in her, there's no doubt in my mind she's got some Chippewa. How else would you explain the way she'll be sitting there, in front of her TV story, rocking in her armchair and suddenly she turns on me, her brown eyes hard as lake-bed flint.

"Lipsha Morrissey," she'll say, "you went out last night and got drunk."

How did she know that? I'll hardly remember it myself. Then she'll say she just had a feeling or ache in the scar of her hand or a creak in her shoulder. She is constantly being told things by little aggravations in her joints or by her household appliances. One time she told Gordie never to ride with a crazy Lamartine boy. She had seen something in the polished-up tin of her bread toaster. So he didn't. Sure enough, the time came we heard how Lyman and Henry went out of control in their car, ending up in the river. Lyman swam to the top, but Henry never made it.

Thanks to Grandma's toaster, Gordie was probably spared.

Someplace in the blood Grandma Kashpaw knows things. She also remembers things, I found. She keeps things filed away. She's got a memory like them video games that don't forget your score. One reason she remembers so many details about the trouble I gave her in early life is so she can flash back her total when she needs to.

Like now. Take the love medicine. I don't know where she remembered that from. It came tumbling from her mind like an asteroid off the corner of the screen.

Of course she starts out by mentioning the time I had this accident in church and did she leave me there with wet overhalls? No she didn't. And ain't I glad? Yes I am. Now what you want now, Grandma?

But when she mentions them love medicines, I feel my back prickle at the danger. These love medicines is something of an old

Chippewa specialty. No other tribe has got them down so well. But love medicines is not for the layman to handle. You don't just go out and get one without paying for it. Before you get one, even, you should go through one hell of a lot of mental condensation. You got to think it over. Choose the right one. You could really mess up your life grinding up the wrong little thing.

So anyhow, I said to Grandma I'd give this love medicine some thought. I knew the best thing was to go ask a specialist like Old Man Pillager, who lives up in a tangle of bush and never shows himself. But the truth is I was afraid of him, like everyone else. He was known for putting the twisted mouth on people, seizing up their hearts. Old Man Pillager was serious business, and I have always thought it best to steer clear of that whenever I could. That's why I took the powers in my own hands. That's why I did what I could.

I put my whole mentality to it, nothing held back. After a while I started to remember things I'd heard gossiped over.

I heard of this person once who carried a charm of seeds that looked like baby pearls. They was attracted to a metal knife, which made them powerful. But I didn't know where them seeds grew. Another love charm I heard about I couldn't go along with, because how was I suppose to catch frogs in the act, which it required. Them little creatures is slippery and fast. And then the powerfullest of all, the most extreme, involved nail clips and such. I wasn't anywhere near asking Grandma to provide me all the little body bits that this last love recipe called for. I went walking around for days just trying to think up something that would work.

Well I got it. If it hadn't been the early fall of the year, I never would have got it. But I was sitting underneath a tree one day down near the school just watching people's feet go by when something tells me, look up! Look up! So I look up, and I see two honkers, Canada geese, the kind with little masks on their faces, a bird what mates for life. I see them flying right over my head naturally preparing to land in some slough on the reservation, which they certainly won't get off of alive.

It hits me, anyway. Them geese, they mate for life. And I think to myself, just what if I went out and got a pair? And just what if I fed some part—say the goose heart—of the female to Grandma and Grandpa ate the other heart? Wouldn't that work? Maybe it's all invisible, and then maybe again it's magic. Love is a stony road. We know that for sure. If it's true that the higher feelings of devotion get lodged in the heart like people say, then we'd be home free. If not, eating goose heart couldn't harm nobody anyway. I thought it was worth my effort, and Grandma Kashpaw thought so, too. She had always known a good idea when she heard one. She borrowed me Grandpa's gun.

So I went out to this particular slough, maybe the exact same slough I never got thrown in by my mother, thanks to Grandma Kashpaw, and I hunched down in a good comfortable pile of rushes. I got my gun loaded up. I ate a few of these soft baloney sandwiches Grandma made me for lunch. And then I waited. The cattails blown back and forth above my head. Them stringy blue herons was spearing up their prey. The thing I know how to do best in this world, the thing I been training for all my life, is to wait. Sitting there and sitting there was no hardship on me. I got to thinking about some funny things that happened. There was this one time that Lulu Lamartine's little blue tweety bird, a paraclete, I guess you'd call it, flown up inside her dress and got lost within there. I recalled her running out into the hallway trying to yell something, shaking. She was doing a right good jig there, cutting the rug for sure, and the thing is it *never* flown out. To this day people speculate where it went. They fear she might perhaps of crushed it in her corsets. It sure hasn't ever yet been seen alive. I thought of funny things for a while, but then I used them up, and strange things that happened started weaseling their way into my mind.

I got to thinking quite naturally of the Lamartine's cousin named Wristwatch. I never knew what his real name was. They called him Wristwatch because he got his father's broken wristwatch as a young boy when his father passed on. Never in his whole life did Wristwatch take his father's watch off. He didn't care if it worked, although after a while he got sensitive when people asked what time it was, teasing him. He often put it to his ear like he was listening to the tick. But it was broken for good and forever, people said so, at least that's what they thought.

Well I saw Wristwatch smoking in his pickup one afternoon and by nine that evening he was dead.

He died sitting at the Lamartine's table, too. As she told it, Wristwatch had just eaten himself a good-size dinner and she said would he take seconds on the hot dish when he fell over to the floor. They turnt him over. He was gone. But here's the strange thing: when the Senior Citizens' orderly took the pulse he noticed that the wristwatch Wristwatch wore was now working. The moment he died the wristwatch started keeping perfect time. They buried him with the watch still ticking on his arm.

I got to thinking. What if some gravediggers dug up Wristwatch's casket in two hundred years and that watch was still going? I thought what question they would ask and it was this: Whose hand wound it?

I started shaking like a piece of grass at just the thought.

Not to get off the subject or nothing, I was still hunkered in the slough. It was passing late into the afternoon and still no honkers had touched down. Now I don't need to tell you that the waiting did not get to me, it was the chill. The rushes was very soft, but damp. I was getting cold and debating to leave, when they landed. Two geese swimming here and there as big as life, looking deep into each other's little pinhole eyes. Just the ones I was looking for. So I lifted Grandpa's gun to my shoulder and I aimed perfectly, and *blam! Blam!* I delivered two accurate shots. But the thing is, them shots missed. I couldn't hardly believe it. Whether it was that the stock had warped or the barrel got bent someways, I don't quite know, but anyway them geese flown off into the dim sky, and Lipsha Morrissey was left there in the rushes with evening fallen and his two cold hands empty. He had before him just the prospect of another day of bone-cracking chill in them rushes, and the thought of it got him depressed.

Now it isn't my style, in no way, to get depressed.

So I said to myself, Lipsha Morrissey, you're a happy S.O.B. who could be covered up with weeds by now down at the bottom of this slough, but instead you're alive to tell the tale. You might have problems in life, but you still got the touch. You got the power, Lipsha Morrissey. Can't argue that. So put your mind to it and figure out how not to be depressed.

I took my advice. I put my mind to it. But I never saw at the time how my thoughts led me astray toward a tragic outcome none could have known. I ignored all the danger, all the limits, for I was tired of sitting in the slough and my feet were numb. My face was aching. I was chilled, so I played with fire. I told myself love medicine was simple. I told myself the old superstitions was just that—strange beliefs. I told myself to take the ten dollars Mary MacDonald had paid me for putting the touch on her arthritis joint, and the other five I hadn't spent yet from winning bingo last Thursday. I told myself to go down to the Red Owl store.

And here is what I did that made the medicine backfire. I took an evil shortcut. I looked at birds that was dead and froze.

All right. So now I guess you will say, "Slap a malpractice suit on Lipsha Morrissey."

I heard of those suits. I used to think it was a color clothing quack doctors had to wear so you could tell them from the good ones. Now I know better that it's law.

As I walked back from the Red Owl with the rock-hard, heavy turkeys, I argued to myself about malpractice. I thought of faith. I thought to myself that faith could be called belief against the odds and whether or not there's any proof. How does that sound? I thought how we might have to yell to be heard by Higher Power, but that's not saying it's not *there*. And that is faith for you. It's belief even when the goods don't deliver. Higher Power makes promises we all know they can't back up, but anybody ever go and slap an old malpractice suit on God? Or the U.S. government? No they don't. Faith might be stupid, but it gets us through. So what I'm heading at is this. I finally convinced myself that the real actual power to the love medicine was not the goose heart itself but the faith in the cure.

I didn't believe it, I knew it was wrong, but by then I had waded so far into my lie I was stuck there. And then I went one step further.

The next day, I cleaned the hearts away from the paper packages of gizzards inside the turkeys. Then I wrapped them hearts with a clean hankie and brung them both to get blessed up at the mission. I wanted to get official blessings from the priest, but when Father answered the door to the rectory, wiping his hands on a little towel, I could tell he was a busy man.

"Booshoo, Father," I said. "I got a slight request to make of you this afternoon."

"What is it?" he said.

"Would you bless this package?" I held out the hankie with the hearts tied inside it.

He looked at the package, questioning it.

"It's turkey hearts," I honestly had to reply.

A look of annoyance crossed his face.

"Why don't you bring this matter over to Sister Martin," he said. "I have duties."

And so, although the blessing wouldn't be as powerful, I went over to the Sisters with the package.

I rung the bell, and they brought Sister Martin to the door. I had her as a music teacher, but I was always so shy then. I never talked out loud. Now, I had grown taller than Sister Martin. Looking down, I saw that she was not feeling up to snuff. Brown circles hung under her eyes.

"What's the matter?" she said, not noticing who I was.

"Remember me, Sister?"

She squinted up at me.

"Oh yes," she said after a moment. "I'm sorry, you're the youngest of the Kashpaws. Gordie's brother."

Her face warmed up.

"Lipsha," I said, "that's my name."

"Well, Lipsha," she said, smiling broad at me now, "what can I do for you?"

They always said she was the kindest-hearted of the Sisters up the hill, and she was. She brought me back into their own kitchen and made me take a big yellow wedge of cake and a glass of milk.

"Now tell me," she said, nodding at my package. "What have you got wrapped up so carefully in those handkerchiefs?"

Like before, I answered honestly.

"Ah," said Sister Martin. "Turkey hearts." She waited.

"I hoped you could bless them."

She waited some more, smiling with her eyes. Kindhearted though she was, I began to sweat. A person could not pull the wool down over Sister Martin. I stumbled through my mind for an explanation, quick, that wouldn't scare her off.

"They're a present," I said, "for Saint Kateri's statue."

"She's not a saint yet."

"I know," I stuttered on, "in the hopes they will crown her."

"Lipsha," she said, "I never heard of such a thing."

So I told her. "Well the truth is," I said, "it's a kind of medicine."

"For what?"

"Love."

"Oh Lipsha," she said after a moment, "you don't need any medicine. I'm sure any girl would like you exactly the way you are."

I just sat there. I felt miserable, caught in my pack of lies.

"Tell you what," she said, seeing how bad I felt, "my blessing won't make any difference anyway. But there is something you can do."

I looked up at her, hopeless.

"Just be yourself."

I looked down at my plate. I knew I wasn't much to brag about right then, and I shortly became even less. For as I walked out the door I stuck my fingers in the cup of holy water that was sacred from their touches. I put my fingers in and blessed the hearts, quick, with my own hand.

I went back to Grandma and sat down in her little kitchen at the Senior Citizens. I unwrapped them hearts on the table, and her hard agate eyes went soft. She said she wasn't even going to cook those hearts up but eat them raw so their power would go down strong as possible.

I couldn't hardly watch when she munched hers. Now that's true love. I was worried about how she would get Grandpa to eat his, but she told me she'd think of something and don't worry. So I did not. I was supposed to hide off in her bedroom while she put dinner on a plate for Grandpa and fixed up the heart so he'd eat it. I caught a glint of the plate she was making for him. She put that heart smack on a piece of lettuce like in a restaurant and then attached to it a little heap of boiled peas.

He sat down. I was listening in the next room.

She said, "Why don't you have some mash potato?" So he had some mash potato. Then she gave him a little piece of boiled meat. He ate that. Then she said, "Why you didn't never touch your salad yet. See that heart? I'm feeding you it because the doctor said your blood needs building up."

I couldn't help it, at that point I peeked through a crack in the door.

I saw Grandpa picking at that heart on his plate with a certain look. He didn't look appetized at all, is what I'm saying. I doubted our plan was going to work. Grandma was getting worried, too. She told him one more time, loudly, that he had to eat that heart.

"Swallow it down," she said. "You'll hardly notice it."

He just looked at her straight on. The way he looked at her made me think I was going to see the smokescreen drop a second time, and sure enough it happened.

"What you want me to eat this for so bad?" he asked her uncannily.

Now Grandma knew the jig was up. She knew that he knew she was working medicine. He put his fork down. He rolled the heart around his saucer plate.

"I don't want to eat this," he said to Grandma. "It don't look good."

"Why it's fresh grade-A," she told him. "One hundred percent."

He didn't ask percent what, but his eyes took on an even more warier look.

"Just go on and try it," she said, taking the salt shaker in her hand. She was getting annoyed. "Not tasty enough? You want me to salt it for you?" She waved the shaker over his plate.

"All right, skinny white girl!" She had got Grandpa mad. Oopsy-daisy, he popped the heart into his mouth. I was about to yawn loudly and come out of the bedroom. I was about ready for this crash of wills to be over, when I saw he was still up to his old tricks. First he rolled it into one side of his cheek. "Mmmmm," he said. Then he rolled it into the other side of his cheek. "Mmm-mmmm," again. Then he stuck his tongue out with the heart on it and put it back, and there was no time to react. He had pulled Grandma's leg once too far. Her goat was got. She was so mad she hopped up quick as a wink and slugged him between the shoulderblades to make him swallow.

Only thing is, he choked.

He choked real bad. A person can choke to death. You ever sit down at a restaurant table and up above you there is a list of instructions what to do if something slides down the wrong pipe? It sure makes you chew slow, that's for damn sure. When Grandpa fell off his chair better believe me that little graphic illustrated poster fled into my mind. I jumped out the bedroom. I done everything within my power that I could do to unlodge what was choking him. I squeezed underneath his ribcage. I socked him in the back. I was desperate. But here's the factor of decision: he wasn't choking on the heart alone. There was more to it than that. It was other things that choked him as well. It didn't seem like he wanted to struggle or fight. Death came and tapped his chest, so he went just like that. I'm sorry all through my body at what I done to him with that heart, and there's those who will say Lipsha Morrissey is just excusing himself off the hook by giving song and dance about how Grandpa gave up.

Maybe I can't admit what I did. My touch had gone worthless, that is true. But here is what I seen while he lay in my arms.

You hear a person's life will flash before their eyes when they're in danger. It was him in danger, not me, but it was *his* life come over me. I saw him dying, and it was like someone pulled the shade down in a room. His eyes clouded over and squeezed shut, but just before that I looked in. He was still fishing in the middle of Lake Turcot. Big thoughts was on his line and he had half a case of beer in the boat. He waved at me, grinned, and then the bobber went under.

Grandma had gone out of the room crying for help. I bunched my force up in my hands and I held him. I was so wound up I couldn't even breathe. All the moments he had spent with me, all the times he had hoisted me on his shoulders or pointed into the leaves was concentrated in that moment. Time was flashing back and forth like a pinball machine. Lights blinked and balls hopped and rubber bands chirped, until suddenly I realized the last ball had gone down the drain and there was nothing. I felt his force leaving him, flowing out of Grandpa never to return. I felt his mind weakening. The bobber going under in the lake. And I felt the touch retreat back into the darkness inside my body, from where it came.

One time, long ago, both of us were fishing together. We caught a big old snapper what started towing us around like it was a motor. "This here fishline is pretty damn good," Grandpa said. "Let's keep this turtle on and see where he takes us." So we rode along behind that turtle, watching as from time to time it surfaced. The thing was just about the size of a washtub. It took us all around the lake twice, and as it was traveling, Grandpa said something as a joke. "Lipsha," he said, "we are glad your mother didn't want you because we was always looking for a boy like you who would tow us around the lake."

"I ain't no snapper. Snappers is so stupid they stay alive when their head's chopped off," I said.

"That ain't stupidity," said Grandpa. "Their brain's just in their heart, like yours is."

When I looked up, I knew the fuse had blown between my heart and my mind and that a terrible understanding was to be given.

Grandma got back into the room and I saw her stumble. And then she went down too. It was like a house you can't hardly believe has stood so long, through years of record weather, suddenly goes down in the worst yet. It makes sense, is what I'm saying, but you still can't hardly believe it. You think a person you know has got through death and illness and being broke and living on commodity rice will get through anything. Then they fold and you see how fragile were the stones that underpinned them. You see how instantly the ground can shift you thought was solid. You see the stop signs and the yellow dividing markers of roads you traveled and all the instructions you had played according to vanish. You see how all the everyday things you counted on was just a dream you had been having by which you run your whole life. She had been over me, like a sheer overhang or rock dividing Lipsha Morrissey from outer space. And now she went underneath. It was as though the banks gave way on the shores of Lake Turcot, and where Grandpa's passing was just the bobber swallowed under by his biggest thought, her fall was the house and the rock under it sliding after, sending half the lake splashing up to the clouds.

Where there was nothing.

You play them games never knowing what you see. When I fell into the dream alongside of both of them I saw that the dominions I had defended myself from anciently was but delusions of the screen. Blips of light. And I was scot-free now, whistling through space.

I don't know how I come back. I don't know from where. They was slapping my face when I arrived back at Senior Citizens and they was oxygenating her. I saw her chest move, almost unwilling. She sighed the way she would when somebody bothered her in the middle of a row of beads she was counting. I think it irritated her to no end that they brought her back. I knew from the way she looked after they took the mask off, she was not going to forgive them disturbing her restful peace. Nor was she forgiving Lipsha Morrissey. She had been stepping out onto the road of death, she told the children later at the funeral. I asked was there any stop signs or dividing markers on that road, but she clamped her lips in a vise the way she always done when she was mad.

Which didn't bother me. I knew when things had cleared out she wouldn't have no choice. I was not going to speculate where the blame was put for Grandpa's death. We was in it together. She had slugged him between the shoulders. My touch had failed him, never to return.

All the blood children and the took-ins, like me, came home from Minneapolis and Chicago, where they had relocated years ago. They stayed with friends on the reservation or with Aurelia or slept on Grandma's floor. They were struck down with grief and bereavement to be sure, every one of them. At the funeral I sat down in the back of the church with Albertine. She had gotten all skinny and ragged haired from cramming all her years of study into two or three. She had decided that to be a nurse was not enough for her so she was going to be a doctor. But the way she was straining her mind didn't look too hopeful. Her eyes were bloodshot from driving and crying. She took my hand. From the back we watched all the children and the mourners as they hunched over their prayers, their hands stuffed full of Kleenex. It was someplace in that long sad service that my vision shifted. I began to see things different, more clear. The family kneeling down turned to rocks in a field. It struck me how strong and reliable grief was, and death. Until the end of time, death would be our rock.

So I had perspective on it all, for death gives you that. All the Kashpaw children had done various things to me in their lives— shared their folks with me, loaned me cash, beat me up in secret— and I decided, because of death, then and there I'd call it quits. If I ever saw King again, I'd shake his hand. Forgiving somebody else made the whole thing easier to bear.

Everybody saw Grandpa off into the next world. And then the Kashpaws had to get back to their jobs, which was numerous and impressive. I had a few beers with them and I went back to Grandma, who had sort of got lost in the shuffle of everybody being sad about Grandpa and glad to see one another.

Zelda had sat beside her the whole time and was sitting with her now. I wanted to talk to Grandma, say how sorry I was, that it wasn't her fault, but only mine. I would have, but Zelda gave me one of her looks of strict warning as if to say, "I'll take care of Grandma. Don't horn in on the women."

If only Zelda knew, I thought, the sad realities would change her. But of course I couldn't tell the dark truth.

It was evening, late. Grandma's light was on underneath a crack in the door. About a week had passed since we buried Grandpa. I knocked first but there wasn't no answer, so I went right in. The door was unlocked. She was there but she didn't notice me at first.

Her hands were tied up in her rosary, and her gaze was fully absorbed in the easy chair opposite her, the one that had always been Grandpa's favorite. I stood there, staring with her, at the little green nubs in the cloth and plastic armrest covers and the sad little hair-tonic stain he had made on the white doily where he laid his head. For the life of me I couldn't figure what she was staring at. Thin space. Then she turned.

"He ain't gone yet," she said.

Remember that chill I luckily didn't get from waiting in the slough? I got it now. I felt it start from the very center of me, where fear hides, waiting to attack. It spiraled outward so that in minutes my fingers and teeth were shaking and clattering. I knew she told the truth. She seen Grandpa. Whether or not he had been there is not the point. She had *seen* him, and that meant anybody else could see him, too. Not only that but, as is usually the case with these here ghosts, he had a certain uneasy reason to come back. And of course Grandma Kashpaw had scanned it out.

I sat down. We sat together on the couch watching his chair out of the corner of our eyes. She had found him sitting in his chair when she walked in the door.

"It's the love medicine, my Lipsha," she said. "It was stronger than we thought. He came back even after death to claim me to his side."

I was afraid. "We shouldn't have tampered with it," I said. She agreed. For a while we sat still. I don't know what she thought, but my head felt screwed on backward. I couldn't accurately consider the situation, so I told Grandma to go to bed. I would sleep on the couch keeping my eye on Grandpa's chair. Maybe he would come back and maybe he wouldn't. I guess I feared the one as much as the other, but I got to thinking, see, as I lay there in darkness, that perhaps even through my terrible mistakes some good might come. If Grandpa did come back, I thought he'd return in his right mind. I could talk with him. I could tell him it was all my fault for playing with power I did not understand. Maybe he'd forgive me and rest in peace. I hoped this. I calmed myself and waited for him all night.

He fooled me though. He knew what I was waiting for, and it

wasn't what he was looking to hear. Come dawn I heard a blood-splitting cry from the bedroom and I rushed in there. Grandma turnt the lights on. She was sitting on the edge of the bed and her face looked harsh, pinched-up, gray.

"He was here," she said. "He came and laid down next to me in bed. And he touched me."

Her heart broke down. She cried. His touch was so cold. She laid back in bed after a while, as it was morning, and I went to the couch. As I lay there, falling asleep, I suddenly felt Grandpa's presence and the barrier between us like a swollen river. I felt how I had wronged him. How awful was the place where I had sent him. Behind the wall of death, he'd watched the living eat and cry and get drunk. He was lonesome, but I understood he meant no harm.

"Go back," I said to the dark, afraid and yet full of pity. "You got to be with your own kind now," I said. I felt him retreating, like a sigh, growing less. I felt his spirit as it shrunk back through the walls, the blinds, the brick courtyard of Senior Citizens. "Look up Aunt June," I whispered as he left.

I slept late the next morning, a good hard sleep allowing the sun to rise and warm the earth. It was past noon when I awoke. There is nothing, to my mind, like a long sleep to make those hard decisions that you neglect under stress of wakefulness. Soon as I woke up that morning, I saw exactly what I'd say to Grandma. I had gotten humble in the past week, not just losing the touch but getting jolted into the understanding that would prey on me from here on out. Your life feels different on you, once you greet death and understand your heart's position. You wear your life like a garment from the mission bundle sale ever after—lightly because you realize you never paid nothing for it, cherishing because you know you won't ever come by such a bargain again. Also you have the feeling someone wore it before you and someone will after. I can't explain that, not yet, but I'm putting my mind to it.

"Grandma," I said, "I got to be honest about the love medicine."

She listened. I knew from then on she would be listening to me the way I had listened to her before. I told her about the turkey hearts and how I had them blessed. I told her what I used as love medicine was purely a fake, and then I said to her what my understanding brought me.

"Love medicine ain't what brings him back to you, Grandma. No, it's something else. He loved you over time and distance, but he went off so quick he never got the chance to tell you how he loves you, how he doesn't blame you, how he understands. It's true feeling, not no magic. No supermarket heart could have brung him back."

She looked at me. She was seeing the years and days I had no way of knowing, and she didn't believe me. I could tell this. Yet a look came on her face. It was like the look of mothers drinking sweetness from their children's eyes. It was tenderness.

"Lipsha," she said, "you was always my favorite."

She took the beads off the bedpost, where she kept them to say at night, and she told me to put out my hand. When I did this, she shut the beads inside of my fist and held them there a long minute, tight, so my hand hurt. I almost cried when she did this. I don't really know why. Tears shot up behind my eyelids, and yet it was nothing. I didn't understand, except her hand was so strong, squeezing mine.

The earth was full of life and there was dandelions growing out the window, thick as thieves, already seeded, fat as big yellow plungers. She let my hand go. I got up. "I'll go out and dig a few dandelions," I told her.

Outside, the sun was hot and heavy as a hand on my back. I felt it flow down my arms, out my fingers, arrowing through the ends of the fork into the earth. With every root I prized up there was return, as if I was kin to its secret lesson. The touch got stronger as I worked through the grassy afternoon. Uncurling from me like a seed out of the blackness where I was lost, the touch spread. The spiked leaves full of bitter mother's milk. A buried root. A nuisance people dig up and throw in the sun to wither. A globe of frail seeds that's indestructible.

MICHAEL DORRIS

Michael Dorris was born in Dayton, Washington, in 1945. He is Modoc. He attended Georgetown and Yale, where he received his B.A. and M.A., respectively, and taught anthropology and Native American studies at Dartmouth. He is married to Louise Erdrich.

Trained as an anthropologist, Dorris is the only writer in this anthology who is not a poet. His nonfiction includes *Native Americans: Five Hundred Years After* (1975) and *The Broken Cord* (1989), a memoir of his relationship with his adopted son, a victim of fetal alcohol syndrome. *The Broken Cord* won the National Book Critics' Award.

"Rayona's Seduction," two chapters from Dorris's novel, *A Yellow Raft in Blue Water* (1987), is about a teenage mixed-blood girl, half Indian, half black. Dorris presents a keen tragicomic portrait of a girl who can't seem to win for losing. Abandoned by her father and mother, ignored by the grandmother with whom she goes to live, and taunted by her Indian peers because she looks black, Rayona is befriended by a priest who eventually assaults her sexually.

"Rayona's Seduction" raises some issues about ethnic identity that we haven't seen before. American attitudes toward different ethnic groups are inconsistent. If someone is half or quarter Indian—has one Indian parent or grandparent—but half or three-quarters white, he or she often has a hard time establishing Indian identity. On the other hand, if an American has any recognizable black features, he or she is black, period. For ethnic purposes there are no black mixed-bloods in this country, no mulattoes, anymore. Rayona has great difficulty claiming her Indian heritage because to the Indians of her mother's tribe she is simply black.

Dorris is adept at portraying subtleties and inconsistencies in attitudes about ethnicity and at depicting the blending of cultures. Rayona's grandmother will speak only "Indian" to Rayona but spends her day watching "As the World Turns" and "The People's Court" on television.

Aunt Ida and I don't know what to do with each other. We are unexpected surprises, spoiled plans, bad luck. We bump against each other in the three rooms of her house, four if you count the bathroom that doesn't work. Aunt Ida sleeps propped on a studio couch in the small bedroom, her head and back against a mountain of pillows crocheted and knitted into the lumpy shapes of dull-colored small animals. Against one wall of the living room, lined in a row facing the outer door, are the cookstove, washing machine, and television, and just beside the set of wooden stairs leading to the attic leans the refrigerator. Spotting its white surface are yellow magnets, each printed in the shape of a Happy Face with HAVE A NICE DAY written around the edges. I thought they might be arranged in some pattern I could figure out, but I finally gave up and asked Aunt Ida.

"They come in my cereal," she said. "Plastic crap to hold grocery lists. I save them for Bingo covers."

Water is a problem at Aunt Ida's house this summer. There isn't any most of the time, thanks to a dry spell that has depleted the runoff into the dug well. Twice a week—more often now that I'm here using it too, Aunt Ida reminds me—she walks to her neighbor's creek, fills a red twenty-five-gallon plastic jug and hauls it back to live off. Between uses, the jug is stored in the sink, ready for when a cup needs washing or when your hands are dirty. The drain still works fine. There are stacked boxes in the kitchen area and on the attic stairs, filled like shelves with dried and preserved food—commodity peanut butter and powdered eggs and canned lard. I ask her about that too, why she hoards so much, but even before the words are out of my mouth I see a box of kindling and remember what Mom always said about the winters in Montana and how they made her glad to be in Seattle no matter how rotten things got. During the long, dark blizzards Aunt Ida's house would be cut off for days from everywhere in the world. There's no way she'd want to depend on electricity, a BIA check, or the reservation store.

I have the room that was once Mom's, and when my jeans get too dirty, I wear any of her teenage clothes that I can squeeze into: green pedal pushers and patched white socks and a Bobby Rydell sweat shirt. Still tacked to her wall are pictures of Elvis Presley, Jacqueline Kennedy, and Connie Francis, and on the sagging shelf in the closet, piles of red and blue and yellow high-school note-books. Each one is labeled on the cover—Religion or English or Civics—but inside there is no work, just a page or two of Mom's drawings of faces and horses and zigzaggy beadwork designs, and long lists of her name, written in purple ink with all the I's dotted with hearts: "Mrs. Christine Doney. Mrs. Christine Presley. Mrs. Christine LaVallee. Mrs. Christine Garcia."

In a box under the bed is an album still wrapped in cellophane and piles of loose pictures of Mom, school portraits, snapshots with her friends, an eighty-by-ten graduation photo in color. In that one, her head is turned back toward the camera. She is posed like a saint that I recognize from a painting in church. I forget who, some Lucy or Bernadette or somebody having a vision. Her eyes are lifted up and a light shines on her hair and forehead. Her lips have been carefully colored in with a red marker. She wears a white blouse that's pinned at the neck with a silver-and-turquoise circle that Mom still wears for special.

When I come across that picture I can barely look at it. I slam the lid of the box shut and push it under the bed. But five minutes later I take it out and study every detail. I try to see a resemblance, some-thing in me that looks like her at my age. I even hold the picture to the mirror next to my face and go over it again—hair, eyes, nose, mouth, chin. But she still is Mom and I still am me. She is holy, one step from shooting off to heaven, and I look ready to fight.

Once I read a story in a magazine about how some man from the city came out to a farm and couldn't get to sleep at night because it was too quiet. He would have had no trouble at all at

Aunt Ida's. There is always at least one radio going, and half the time a tape hums in the Walkman. Noise fills the house and squirts outside under all the windows that won't shut flush and through the TV antenna hole in the roof where rain gets in. I swim through commercials and on-the-air auctions and news updates and pick hits like a fish in a crowded dime-store aquarium. In every room my head buzzes with voices twining in Montana accents, and outside the wasps and mosquitoes are so thick that I can't find a place to think. I spend my time reading stories in Mom's old *Seventeen*s and pasting her pictures in the album.

Aunt Ida's real life is squeezed between the times of her programs on TV. She knows and is annoyed with all the characters on "As the World Turns" and never misses an episode. She loses her patience with their ignorance, their slowness to figure out what's happening around them, what plots are taking place. The first few times I heard her yell, "Wake up and see what's before your face!" or "He's just after your money," I thought someone was visiting, but quick enough her voice became part of the background I ignore. Sometimes when things in Oakdale drag, Aunt Ida leaps from her rocker and turns off the sound. She can't stand to hear her people be so dumb.

In the late afternoons she watches Judge Wapner and "The People's Court" and it's even worse. She doesn't trust the men and women who come in to tell their bitching stories. She mimics their words and snorts at their excuses. "Serves you right!" she shouts at the screen. She saves her worst contempt for the judge himself. She doubts his credentials, the existence of his brain. "How'd *you* like to be on the other side sometime?" she asks him when she disagrees with his verdict.

Except for that first afternoon when she held my arms behind my back she hasn't touched me at all, and we don't talk much. She points her fingers at things she wants me to see or do, rolls her eyes when I get it wrong, and shushes me if I interrupt during one of her shows. I am her duty, she says with her long sighs and banged-down plates, but she doesn't have to like it.

I tell myself that it's not me causing Aunt Ida's irritation. Mom's the one that's eating at her, and I'm just the unwelcome reminder, a bad news list stuck under a Happy Face on her refrigerator. Aunt Ida watches me for mistakes, begrudges me the space I take. She follows the same routine of TV and work every day as if her life depended on it, and I am a distraction, a strange-looking unknown relative who fell into her life like something dropped out of an airplane to lighten the load.

On Sundays she insists that I listen with her to a Mass that's broadcast from the Catholic cathedral in Denver.

"I was there once for the feast of Corpus Christi," she told me the day I arrived, when she was still feeling sympathetic and hadn't realized she was stuck with me. "I was a bead in the living rosary at the racetrack, between the first and second joyful mysteries."

Aunt Ida will talk to me only in Indian, though I suspect she knows English. It's a lucky thing Mom always spoke the old language, like a secret code, around the apartment and when she and I were alone together. This was to give me my identity, according to Mom, and thanks to her I can understand Aunt Ida, even if at first I'm too shy in answering.

I decide Aunt Ida made up her story about Denver to seem important, to seem as though she belongs to this big church in Colorado. I think she needs a reason to explain why she stays home and listens to the radio every week instead of going to the Mission church ten miles away. Late one afternoon of the first week I'm there, I hear the sound of a car and sneak a look from my window to see an elderly priest get out of an old pickup with HOLY MARTYRS MISSION stenciled on the side panel. I listen from the bedroom as Aunt Ida stands with him at the front door. He asks in Indian if she has time for a cup of tea.

"I have this girl here," she says, "that I have to watch."

"Is Christine back? Is she with you for long?"

I'm surprised he knows our language, surprised at how much else he seems to know, and I hang on what Aunt Ida will say next. These are questions I want answered.

"Her mother left her. Pauline heard she's over living with Dayton."

Living with Dayton? Here? I thought Mom had gone back to

Seattle, or anywhere away from this reservation. How does Aunt Ida know this? Was it on some radio show I missed?

"And she left her little girl with you? Rayona must be almost grown by now."

Silence.

"Will she be completing her school year at the Mission?"

Before Aunt Ida can answer, if she's going to, I come into the front room. The priest is a short gray-haired man with blue eyes and a big stomach. His skin is weathered and tan against his wrinkled black suit. When he sees me he looks to Aunt Ida in amazement.

"This can't be Rayona."

Aunt Ida has her arms folded across her chest, her feet apart, her eyes directed at the clock on top of the washing machine. "As the World Turns" came on two minutes ago.

The priest turns to me. "My name is Father Hurlburt," he says in English. "I met you as a baby. And of course I remember your mother very well. . . ."

His words slip through my defenses and bring Mom's face to my mind. She appears as she was the morning we left Seattle, tired but satisfied with herself at Village Video. I flash to the bumper sticker on the back of Mom's Volaré.

"I AM CHRISTINE. I AM PURE EVIL," I quote aloud without thinking.

Father Hurlburt grabs his hand to his chest as if he's shocked into a heart attack or else ready to withdraw a crucifix. He thinks I'm a space cadet, but Aunt Ida glances at me and bites on her lip. I've said something she likes, something she doesn't think is dumb. Then her face sets again.

Father Hurlburt lets out his breath and tries to act as if I've made a great joke. "You had me going," he says. "Oh yes, you really took me by surprise." He clears his throat and changes the subject. "This reservation must seem very different from Seattle."

" 'The land of the sky-blue waters,' " I say, taking a line from a commercial that plays all the time. Aunt Ida shoots her glance over at me. This time she actually smiles for a split second before she turns expressionless.

"What would she know? She sits in that room all day." Aunt Ida rolls her eyes in the direction of Mom's door. "She speaks Indian," she adds.

"You're so very tall"—Father Hurlburt switches languages and says to me—"but too thin. Have you made any friends yet around here?" He has not mentioned the color of my skin. I'm supposed to think he hasn't noticed.

I shake my head. I have no friends.

"And you are, what, about sixteen years old?"

"She's fifteen," Aunt Ida says before I can feel good that I look older. It takes me a second to realize she knows my age, that he knew where I was from. I can't imagine that Aunt Ida has ever thought of me or mentioned me before my arrival, but she must have.

"Perfect, perfect." Father Hurlburt rubs his hands together as though he is warming them before a fire. His fingers are stubby and thick. He nods at me while he talks. "We'll enroll you at the Mission high school, starting next week, but in the meantime I know exactly the way for you to get acquainted, provided you have been raised a Catholic?"

"Sort of." Mom pointed me in the direction of Mass most Sundays, sent me to the nuns whenever we were close enough to a Catholic school in Seattle, and trivia-quizzed me on the lives of all the saints, but she never set foot inside a church herself that I can remember.

"Excellent. The God Squad it is, then." He swings his mouth-open smile from Aunt Ida to me and back again. The skin of his face is creased and rolled. He's relieved to know what to do with me, but sees my doubt.

"Don't let the name fool you. It's a nice group of young people, and my new assistant pastor has taken a great interest in the organization. There are weekly meetings and teen dances. Only one retreat a year. St. Dominic Savio is the patron. It's not as bad as I make it sound."

I'm not convinced. I know all about Dominic Savio, the preteen saint. The nuns at my last school in Seattle were crazy about him and had his plaster statue on a pedestal by the door of the classroom. He stood watch above the holy water font, dressed in lemon-yellow pants and a lime sports jacket. In one hand, close to his heart, he clutched a book, a Daily Missal probably, and from the other hand he held up a single finger. The hair on his too-small head was an unnatural black and from his bright red lips he seemed ready to say "No, no" or "Better not." His motto was "Death Rather Than Sin," and he died at twelve. I wait for Aunt Ida to refuse, to tell the priest I can't make it.

"There's only one problem," Father Hurlburt goes on. He reaches inside his coat, pulls out a small pocket calendar, and licks his finger, turning pages until he finds the one he wants. Then he frowns. "I'm so swamped this week! And unfortunately my poor old truck does not have the bi-location!"

Father Hurlburt winks at me as if he has said something cute, and I remember Dominic Savio's trick of being in two places at the same time. Aunt Ida's eyes are focused so hard on the television that I wonder if she can follow her program through the blank screen. Finally she glances over at the priest as he continues to talk to her.

"Either I can have Father Novak stop by for Rayona on Saturday and take her to the God Squad meeting, or we can skip that and I'll run by on Sunday morning and bring you *both* over to Holy Martyrs for eight o'clock Mass."

Two days later I'm sitting in the Mission pickup next to Father Tom Novak on my way to the God Squad. He talks nonstop, as though he's answering the question "Tell me everything about yourself," except I never asked it. He wants me to call him "Father Tom."

"Guess how long I've been here?" he says. He's wearing a big beaded medallion that rides low on his black cassock. He's the kind that wants to be everybody's buddy, the kind they bring in for guitar Masses.

When I don't guess, Father Tom jumps right in. "Two weeks! Imagine, just three weeks ago today I was walking down the street in Milwaukee. I had never been west of Wisconsin!"

I could see him. He'd have his arm bent with his Missal clutched in his hand. His black skirt would swing as he walked and his balding head would shine like it had just been buffed. He'd be looking for people to talk to, to tell how he was all set to come out to Montana and save the Indians.

"I hear you're new in these parts yourself, Rayona," Father Tom says.

I wonder what he's heard, if he knows about Mom or where she is. The ruts in the road are deeper, closer together, than they were with Mom. Green alfafa grows behind wire fences in the leased land along the side, and as the car approaches, two large sea gulls lift slowly, circling overhead until we pass. They have been stabbing at the remains of another bird, struck and flattened by an earlier car. Its one undamaged wing rises straight from the asphalt and moves in the wind, as if to wave us down.

"You don't talk much, do you?" he says. "But that's okay, since I talk enough for an army!"

He is a real jerk, a dork, the kids in Seattle would call him. Somewhere Mom is off having a good time with her old boyfriend. Aunt Ida finally has her house to herself. I imagine that Mom and Dad are the gulls and that I'm driving. I surprise them by gunning the engine and come faster than they expect. They try to flap off sideways to avoid my grill. Their eyes glint, betrayed, scared shitless.

"Here we are." The God Squad meets in the basement of the Mission hall. Father Tom parks the truck and I follow him inside, but he stops to talk to a couple of old men who are sitting on the steps.

"Howdy, Mr. Stiffarm," he says, reaching for and pumping the hand of the nearest one. "I must have missed you at church last Sunday."

The old man's stare is milky as cat's-eye marbles, and when he smiles, I see he has no teeth. He's dressed in a tan-and-black-plaid wool shirt and gray pants. His hair is white and mussed, recently washed.

"This new priest, he's so dumb he thinks I'm Henry Stiffarm," the man says in Indian to his friend, raising his thin eyebrows and pursing his lips. He laughs and nods his head. They ignore me as if I don't exist. They have no idea I understand their words.

"Just lucky for you he doesn't think you are *Annabelle* Stiffarm," the other man answers, all stone-faced. "He might try to convert you then."

That starts the two of them giggling, and Father Tom joins right in, laughing at himself as if this was the funniest thing he'd ever heard. I close my eyes at his stupidity.

The old men are enjoying themselves, but they become quiet in noticing that I've caught their joke. Their vacuum-cleaner eyes scan and study, pulling out information and storing it away. And yet there's no sign of welcome, no softening. I think of a worm's esophagus, stained blue under my microscope in biology class.

"Here's the clubhouse," Father Tom says when we get to the basement. The walls are cement block, painted green, and the floor, littered with Pepsi and 7-Up cans, is concrete. Facing me is a black-and-white poster with Chief Joseph's picture on it and "Indian Pride" printed underneath. Fluorescent lights span the ceiling. A pool table, two broken-down couches, and a garbage can full of empty McDonald's boxes are the only furniture. From an invisible radio, Kool and the Gang sing "Cherish." And sitting on one of the sofas are two of the meanest-looking people I have ever seen. The fact that they are young, not much older than me, the fact that one of them is a girl, is not at all reassuring. I think again about those sea gulls on the road and mentally floor the gas.

The two on the couch look me up and down. I know what they see. Wrong color, outsider, skinny, friend of the priest, friend of the dork.

"Here is a new member," Father Tom says. His voice is loud and blasts into the dim room. "Her name is Rayona and she's here visiting all the way from Seattle, Washington."

The girl laughs into her hand, and pushes the boy's side with her elbow. Her long black hair is teased into a rat's nest and she wears tight jeans, a cowboy shirt, and too much eyeliner.

"This is Annabelle Stiffarm," Father Tom says. "She's one of the founders of the God Squad and a senior in the Honor Society at the Mission school."

Annabelle tries to look at me but I am too funny. She laughs harder, finally calming herself by taking a package of extra-long Salems out of her fringed and dirty brown leather purse and lighting up. She has a hard time.

"This is Kennedy Cree, but everybody calls him Foxy." Father Tom grins at the boy, who looks like a snake turned into a human being. Not that he isn't good-looking. His black hair falls over his forehead, and his coal eyes paralyze me. "I know who you are," he says.

There's something in the way he looks at me that makes me feel ugly, off-balance, and it shocks me. It's like sticking out your hand in the dark and touching something soft and damp. Your stomach sinks and you want to bear back on your neck, hunch up your shoulders. But I don't let on. I ignore him and pretend to read the caption under the Chief Joseph poster as though I had never seen it before.

"You're Christine's kid," he says. "The one whose father is a nigger."

People don't usually come right out and say it, so in a way his words are a relief. If that's the worst he can do, it's not so bad.

"We're cousins," he goes on. "My mom is Pauline, Aunt Ida's younger sister. They're real close. Of course my mom had a husband."

I've relaxed too soon. He's trying for a way to get to me, trying to impress this Annabelle, who's laughing so hard now I think she'll beat her head on the wall.

"Foxy!" Father Tom says.

He's coming to my rescue. He doesn't know enough to keep quiet, to let the words wash over without snagging.

"That's no way to talk, especially here. I persuaded Rayona to join us because she's alone and needs some friends her own age. I am highly disappointed in you."

Foxy reaches over to put his hand on the back of Annabelle's neck. I think he's gentle with her but then I see his muscles tense, his fingers squeeze and dig. Her laughter stops. She twists her head, ready to let him have it, but when she sees his eyes, cold and flat, she changes her mind. He releases her, and she rubs the base of her skull in resentment.

"Rayona doesn't care," Foxy says. "She's *glad* to meet her full-blood cousin."

They all look at me. What do I say? What do I do not to be dumb? I do the safest thing. I pretend that everything's fine. I smile out of the corner of my mouth and nod my head at Foxy. I'm offering to side with him and Annabelle and cut loose of Father Tom. Us together. Everybody understands what's happening except the priest. He thinks his plan has worked. But we know different. They can take me or leave me. If they take me, I'll be the butt of jokes, the one they dump on. If they leave me, it means I'm not even good enough for that.

They leave me.

"We've got to be somewhere," Foxy says. He motions Annabelle to her feet and pushes at her back as he heads for the stairs.

They could ask me to come along. They don't. They could at least say good-bye, something mean, that would give me a place. They don't. They walk up the steps. Foxy's voice, a mumble I can't understand, drifts back, followed by wild laughter from Annabelle and the slam of the outside door. I am their fool, the thing to tell other people.

Father Tom and I sit on the couch and wait an hour for more members of the God Squad to arrive. Finally, he drives me back to Aunt Ida's. He's sorry. There is a lot going on today, probably. Next time will be different. I'll see. I shouldn't be discouraged. Foxy is really a nice young man and Annabelle and I will become great friends.

When I walk through the door, Aunt Ida is involved in "The People's Court." A woman claims that a man promised to groom her dog and then clipped it too short. She wants a hundred dollars for her anguish. Judge Wapner laughs in her face. He said the dog isn't even a purebreed. The man gets off free and the woman is mad but still glad to be on television. Aunt Ida is disgusted with all of them. She says they waste her time with their fighting. She doesn't ask about my meeting and I go back to Mom's room. Radio music seeps under my door. On the wall, Connie Francis and Elvis Presley flirt at each other. I open the album and look at Mom's smiling mouth.

It's clear that I'll wind up Father Tom's favorite. There's no avoiding it. Mom is gone and Aunt Ida barely pays attention to me. I'm on my own and it's just a matter of time until Father Tom decides I'm his special project. There's no one to stand in his way.

Only four weeks of school remain, but I have to go anyway. I'm in a class of twelve people, one of them Annabelle. They have heard about me before I enroll and don't take any chances by being friendly. I'm taller than any of them, and darker. I wear Mom's twenty-year-old clothes, which, no matter how much Aunt Ida springs the seams and rips the hems, are still too tight, too short. I look ridiculous, like someone who grew overnight, or I look like a boy. Aunt Ida's sister, Pauline, feels sorry for me and sends over hand-me-downs, things Foxy doesn't want. This gives him another thing to laugh at. I make my mind a blank, and the nuns have to call on me twice before I hear them.

My school in Seattle was better than the Mission, and I know more than anyone expects. The nuns call the principal where I used to go and find out that I have good grades, that I have potential. They announce this news to the class, and the other students look at me as if I come from Mars. I don't care. I do no work, but the nuns praise me anyway. They read my papers aloud to show how smart I am. They pin my tests to the bulletin board. This wins me no friends. Annabelle makes sure everybody sees and hears the things I do and that they realize I'm a jerk. I don't care. If anyone looks at me, I duck my head. If anyone talks to me, I frown.

Mom doesn't come by or send word, and there's nobody I can ask about her. I don't know Dayton's last name, and no Daytons exist in Mom's school yearbook.

One day Father Hurlburt brings a brown parcel addressed to Mom. I see it's from Charlene, and remember about the medicine she was going to send. I'm impatient with Aunt Ida, since she leaves the package sitting on the table by her front door and makes no effort that I can see to tell Mom it's here.

"Shouldn't we forward this on?" I say at last. "It might be important." Aunt Ida puffs her cheeks and blows out air.

"I think it's medicine," I say.

But she won't talk about Mom with me and doesn't touch the package. Sometimes I think of it as bait, a piece of ripe meat set in a trap for a hungry animal. Sometimes I think of it as Mom herself, hiding under wraps and watching everything that I do. Having that box in the room makes me feel better, like a promise that might be kept. Sooner or later it will lure Mom. I convince myself that Aunt Ida cannot help but let Mom know. The package is too loud. I pretend to know what's going on and wait out each day, sleep out each night.

Foxy calls me "Buffalo Soldier," after the black men who were cavalry scouts and fought Indians a long time ago. He leaves a note stuck in the Africa section of my geography book. "When are you going home?" it says. Even Manuel Isaacs, who has the blond hair and green eyes of his white mother, takes a shot.

"Hey, Ray," he calls to me one day in earshot of everybody. "You sure you ain't looking for the *Blackfeet* reservation? You must of took a wrong turn."

For sure, there's no avoiding I am going to fall into Father Tom's clutch. I know he's finally taken a bead on me the day he comes to Aunt Ida's and asks me to be his special assistant at the Mission.

"I really need you, Rayona," he says with a big wet smile. He must count me for at least two of those three-hundred-day indulgences each Beatitude is worth. I recognize all the signs. People have taken me under their wings before.

"I don't know how," I tell him, but he says I can learn, he'll teach me.

I admit I gave in without a fight. Father Tom is the last one on the reservation I want to know, but he's the only one who wants to know me. And he needs me more than he thinks.

"I hear you speak your native tongue, Rayona," he says one day after I've arranged the altar for his morning Mass.

Why do they always call it that, "native tongue"?

"My mom is from here." I state a fact he has to know already. "She talked it at home. I can understand it okay."

"I smell like dogshit!" Father Tom booms out at me in Indian. The church echoes with his voice.

I've heard him say this before. Foxy told Annabelle, who couldn't believe her ears that such a hilarious thing had happened, that when Vance Windyboy, on the Tribal Council, found out Father Tom wanted to learn the language, he gave him some private lessons.

"You shouldn't say that," I say. "Vance is pulling your leg."

Father Tom's face sags. He looks like some kid who just dropped his Popsicle in the dirt. "What does it mean?" he demands, but I shake my head.

"Just say *hello*," I tell him, giving him the ordinary word, "if you have to say something."

Hello doesn't sound halfway as interesting as *I smell like dogshit* to Father Tom's ear. He looks at me and doesn't trust me one bit.

"Ask Father Hurlburt," I suggest, but I can tell from Father Tom's expression that this is not the way he wants to go.

"I guess I'm just no good at languages," he says.

However, from then on, he checks most things with me before he leaps, and I get pretty well used to having him around. Sometimes he makes me so nervous I want to run from him. But there's no place to go. And sometimes he's all right, kind of familiar. He comes for me two or three times a week. He asks how I am. He talks to me as if I have sense. He reminds me of social workers back in Seattle, and with them I know the questions and the answers I'm supposed to give.

I become the one loyal member of the God Squad, and some meetings it's just him and me and too much Kool-Aid. Each get-together is supposed to have a theme, but no matter what's scheduled, Father Tom finds a way to talk about sex, which he calls "The Wonders of the Human Body." This is a subject about which I have great curiosity but little know-how. People I've known, kids my age, have gotten mixed up in it already and it seems to change them for the worse. Plus, Mom swears off of it for weeks at a time.

But I can't help thinking that, if I had the opportunity and knew all the facts in advance, I could keep the situation under control.

It's clear that Father Tom is no expert himself, at least as far as girls are concerned, since all his examples have to do with boys.

"At the age of fourteen or fifteen," he tells me one day as we drive back up the hill to Aunt Ida's, "boys begin to have dreams."

This does not strike me as all that amazing.

"Do you ever have them?" he asks, blushing but trying to act as though it's the most innocent question in the world.

At first I think he means medicine dreams, which I have read about and which the old folks say are supposed to come at about my age, at least to boys. They're the kind of dreams that tell you about who you are and what you're supposed to be. Vision quests. I am interested that Father Tom believes in them too.

"Not yet," I say. "They never write about girls getting them. But I dreamed of a bear once two years ago. Do you think that means something?"

We've stopped at Aunt Ida's house, and the truck engine is idling. Father Tom gives me a cross-eyed look.

"No, *dreams*," he says. "About the Wonders of the Human Body."

He means sex. His skin turns splotchy red and he looks like one of those mooseheads that are stuffed with a grin on their face. "Have you had that kind of dream?"

I am so surprised by his question that I say yes, which is dumb to do because he wants to hear what they were about.

"I will understand," he says. "No matter what they are."

"It's bad luck to tell your dreams," I warn him, but he won't stop.

"I can help you, Rayona. You need the guidance of an older friend. You have reached the age of puberty and are turning into a young lady."

I get out of the truck and don't look back. His words lasso me.

"An attractive young lady."

It's the first time since the day Mom split that I think I'm really going to lose it. Something rises inside me so hard I think it will lift me off the ground and ram me into the side of the house. I start to turn and face the truck. But it's in reverse. I hear it back down the hill, whining and clanking over the rough ground. When it hits bottom, before it heads toward the Mission, there is a pause. I know without looking that it's out of sight, that Father Tom can't see me standing here, can't know I'm caught by his words. The horn sounds once, twice, more times in a kind of beat. The tires catch, the truck moves off, and for an instant there is a hole of quiet, a pocket of air without any noise, before the call of radios and televisions and bees and wind rushes in to fill my ears.

As the days get longer and hotter, Foxy starts in about my Copper-tone tan. I've been looking forward to summer vacation as if that would be the end of a bad time and the beginning of something else, but one day I walk Aunt Ida's hill from the schoolbus and it's like a curtain is pulled and there's nothing behind it. I haven't become popular and I haven't turned invisible. I am Father Tom's good deed. The way things stand I have my choice of distracting Aunt Ida all day at her house or of staying out of Annabelle and Foxy's way off her property. Or of leaving altogether.

I'm ready to pack and take my chances. Maybe I can jump the Great Northern back to Seattle and locate some of the kids I used to know. I figure I'll take off school for a day or two to plan this out, but not two hours after classes at the Mission start, who taps at the door but Father Tom. Aunt Ida has gone off to visit her sister, so I come outside to talk to him.

"We missed you in Religion, Rayona," he says.

"I must have slept through the alarm."

"Is something troubling you?"

It has rained the night before and the gravel in front of the house sparkles in the sunlight. The air from the mountains is sharp and dry and the breeze has a bite in it. I don't say anything, just drill the toe of my boot in the ground and wait him out.

"You know you can talk to me, Rayona," he says. He's like some-body who has just sat down to watch his favorite show on TV, who doesn't know what's going to happen next but knows he'll enjoy it. He has on his shiny black pants and a washed-thin T-shirt, with a black windbreaker that says SAINTS on the back in gold writing. He has nicked himself shaving, and the dried blood looks like a vampire has dropped on him in his sleep. His skin is as pale as peeled potatoes, and the little arteries show through under his eyes.

"There's nothing to say," I tell him. "I'm just considering how to get out of here, that's all."

He nods, pretending to take me seriously.

"And where are you off to, if I may ask?"

"Back to Seattle, maybe," I say, and then watch his reaction to this idea. He gives a poker face that says he holds a full house.

"When do you leave?" He's stringing me along good, setting to knock my house of cards out from under me. I can smell his "counseling strategy" a mile off.

"Forget it," I say. "I'll come to school. I'm not going anywhere."

Now he's disappointed. He can't take credit for putting me on the right path. I have caved in too quickly and dodged his influence.

"Tell you what." He acts as if I haven't said anything, as if he still has to turn me around. "Come this weekend I'm borrowing Father Hurlburt's pickup and taking you to Helena. To the Teens for Christ Jamboree. You'll represent our local chapter of the God Squad. There will be hootenannies and rap sessions and even movies in the evenings. What do you say to that?" He cracks the knuckles of his dry spaghetti fingers while he talks.

It's a time of day when nobody makes noise on the reservation. People who are usually loud are either gone visiting or sleeping it off or sitting in school, so the quiet kind of settles over us as we stand there, him waiting for me to say something and me trying to think what. At least it's somewhere away from here.

"I say all right."

"All *right!*" he repeats, but a lot louder. His TV program has turned out okay after all. I'll be his sitting duck for two days.

"We shall have a chance to *talk*," he says, and reaches out and pats me on the shoulder, and pulls his hand back. He's trying hard.

For the first time since I arrived on the reservation the time passes too quickly. On Friday afternoon Father Tom, dressed in a green Sears short-sleeved Western snap-front shirt and stiff new jeans, pulls beside me in the Mission truck as I walk on the road home from school, and gives the horn three quick taps.

"God Squad Express all set and ready to go, Rayona!" he shouts loud enough for all the other kids to hear. "I've taken care of everything. Hop in!"

I put my head down and step high onto the running board, then swing myself in through the door, but not fast enough. Behind me I hear Annabelle say, "How many sleeping bags you bringing there, Rayona? Two or one?"

Father Tom stops by Aunt Ida's, but the pump has broken again and she's at the creek for water. I go inside for a change of clothes and my heavy coat, and the first thing I see is what's not there. The package addressed to Mom, the package that sat untouched on the table for weeks, has disappeared. And there's only one way it could have left the house. I go into my room, her old room. Maybe she's left me a note.

And she has been there. I know because her senior high school yearbook, the one with no Daytons, is gone from the bureau where I had left it. She's seen my things scattered about. She knows I'm still here. But she didn't wait. Part of me doesn't want to give up, and makes excuses. "She'll be back," it says. "She just didn't want to run into Aunt Ida. Now that she knows you're here . . ." But she knew it. Where else would I be? I have to face it: I'm not as important as some package she needs from Seattle. My presence won't bring her back.

I meet the frozen eyes of Jackie Kennedy, staring from the opposite wall.

I don't have much but I pack everything that's mine and stuff it into the same plastic garbage bag I came with. I don't take Mom's old clothes and Mom's old pictures. But I do throw in the *Little Big Man* and *Christine* tapes Mom dropped during her escape, in case they have a VCR at this Catholic jamboree. Afterward I can sell them for bus fare, or maybe I'll return them to Village Video if I go back to Seattle.

The door's open, letting flies and hornets into the house, and I don't shut it as I come out. I hurry to get away before Aunt Ida comes, before anybody else sees Father Tom and me leave together. He's busy looking at a map he has folded backward. He gives off a tight, clean smell that even the rolled-down windows of the cab can't camouflage. It reminds me of the atmosphere in a dry-cleaning store, stuffy and overheated. His fingernails are bitten short and square.

The truck springs are old and the road is still rutted from the winter runoff, so we bounce our way back to the main state highway. A month ago I was on this same route with no idea what was in store. I don't talk much, just answer Father Tom's questions with a word or two and keep my face in the wind, counting telephone poles along the track. Finally, after about an hour, he snags me.

"What about your parents, Rayona? Your mother and father."

I try to imagine what he's heard.

"My mom's dead," I say right off. I wait for him to contradict me, to tell me where she is, what he knows. But he lets it pass. His eyes don't even stray from the road. Either he's in the dark or he's smarter than I give him credit. My words ring in my ears and it scares me that I've said them. I've never actually thought of Mom dead, not with all the times in the hospital or all the nights she's stayed out so late that I thought of calling the police or listening to the CB emergency frequency on the radio. I think of her laid out like I've seen people at funeral homes. She'd be pretty. I know just which dress she'd want: the royal blue. I get so into my idea of her gone that I'm light-headed, lost. Father Tom has said something I haven't quite heard. He repeats it.

"And your father?"

I think of Dad standing at the foot of Mom's casket, wringing his hands. I zero in to see what he's worn for the occasion, but it's only his mailman's uniform, like always.

"My dad's a pilot. He flies jumbos, all over the world. That's why I can't live with him. But he's planning to get a place, in L.A."

I never told that story before. I don't know where it comes from—the uniform I guess. But it's not bad.

"A pilot?" Father Tom frowns and steers with one hand. "*Where* does he fly?"

"All over. Japan. South America. Switzerland," I say, naming the first places I think of.

Father Tom takes off his sunglasses and gives me the eye so he can judge whether or not I'm telling the truth. I return him one of Dad's looks, my lashes half down, my stare flat steady. He doesn't know what to think.

"I never knew that, Rayona. I didn't know your father was living."

"Oh, he's living, all right," I say. "He's doing great."

That shuts up Father Tom for a good thirty miles. He can't very well ask me if I'm sure. We're climbing into the mountains now and it's getting dark and cold. Finally I have to close the window. The radio's busted, so we just sit there in the dim light of the instrument panel, waiting to get where we're going.

Father Tom can hold it in no longer.

"Is there anything you need to talk to me about?" he asks.

I don't say a word. The cab seems too small a place, his words too loud. I can hear him breathing while he waits for me to answer.

"It's not easy being a young person alone at your age," Father Tom says, "when you're different."

"I'm not different."

"I mean, your dual heritage," he says. "Not that you shouldn't be proud of it." This is the first time he's admitted to my skin color, to the shape of my nose, to the stiff fullness of my hair.

"And . . . you spend a lot of time by yourself. I don't imagine your aunt is the kind of person you can come to with the questions you must have at this time in your life."

"Are we going to drive all night or what?"

"Are your tired? Do you want to stop?" His voice leaps at me like some pent-up dog who's rushed to the end of its chain.

Stopping, being still, seems even worse than to keep going, so I say no, I'm fine.

"You must notice the changes in your body, the coming of your womanhood," Father Tom continues. Against the night sky his head looks like a comic-book drawing, round and bald on a thin neck. "Has anyone talked to you about your puberty?"

"My dad," I say quickly to cut him off. "My dad told me all about it. He talks about it all the time."

Father Tom is stalled for a minute. "I was very much like you when I was a boy. I didn't have a father either. He was killed when I was just a baby and my mother raised me all alone. I lived with her until I went into the seminary in high school."

"That's real bad," I say, "but I have a father." Then, "Why did you go there, to that seminary?"

"I always knew I had a vocation." It's as though he's talking to himself. "So did Mother. There were moments I tried to fight it, but in the end I always felt God's call, and had to respond."

"So you joined? Just like that?"

He remembers that I'm here. "I went in for you, Rayona. I am God's helper."

Off the reservation, alone in the truck, Father Tom is different than he is back home. Here there's nobody to laugh at him. Here I'm the strange one. His voice is smooth, slipping through the darkness. I don't object. I don't know what to say.

"God loves you, Rayona. You are His perfect creation."

Father Tom puts his hand on top of mine where it rests on the car seat. Our hands lie there together for a minute, then he squeezes my fingers and lets go. I tilt my head against the glass of the window and close my eyes, trying to sleep, trying to keep his words, his moist skin, out of my head as the springs bounce up and down and my teeth bang together in the empty night.

"Wake up, cowgirl!" Father Tom shakes my knee.

The car has stopped at a gasoline station across from the Bearpaw Lake State Park main entrance. From the colorless sky, it looks to be about seven A.M., and Father Tom has on his Saints jacket. He's drinking Coke from a can.

"This is the end of the trail for today," he says. "We're close enough to Helena and I've had it. I need rest. The jamboree doesn't start till tomorrow anyway."

He looks half crazy, even paler than usual, and his eyes are all bloodshot from driving through the night. His lips are red too, and there's a black stubble over his cheeks.

"Do you have to use the powder room?" he asks. "It's right over there." He says this as if it's a joke of some kind, as if it's really daring that he can ask me such a personal question.

The rest room is around to the side of the gas station. To get there I walk between two wrecks propped on blocks and past an overflowing trash bucket. The stale piss smell cuts through the morning air, and the toilet is clogged with wadded paper.

There's no mirror to look into but I can feel that my hair has flattened where I slept on it. The cold water tap is broken and runs continuously, so I cup my palms to splash my face and rinse my mouth. I'm surprised at Father Tom's announcement that the Teens for Christ meeting doesn't begin for another day. He was in a rush to leave the reservation and now we have time to kill. What am I supposed to do while he rests?

Back at the car Father Tom has explained to the bored, sleepy service station man that he is a priest, that I'm really a full-blooded Indian, and that we're here at the lake on our way to some weekend R & R in Helena. I can feel the man looking at me, searching for the Indian, and tuning out Father Tom's long string of words. I wonder if he recognizes me from four weeks ago. He's the one who tried to sell Mom four new retread tires and she almost let him. I wonder if her credit card charge has bounced yet, if he'll ask me about it. But he doesn't know me. And he doesn't like Father Tom enough to ask questions.

We follow the signs and come to the campsites. The park has just opened this week and so it's almost deserted, but Father Tom has to look at five or six spots before he finds the one he wants. It's some distance from the others, behind a stand of pine, and bordered by a stream. Without talking much we unroll the sleeping bags, then collect some wood scraps for a fire. Father Tom has thought to bring hot dogs and buns for lunch, and has bought pop at the gas station to drink.

"We'll have a picnic first."

The ground is spongy and damp, and he can't seem to settle down. The bugs are bad—small, stinging insects that whine close to your ear and then veer away before they can be crushed. He swats at his face and tries without success to start the grill. He goes back to the car twice but doesn't find what he's looking for.

"Tell you what. I'm so tired I can't sleep, and it's such a pretty day. Let's get out of these clothes and into our swimming suits. We'll take a dip before lunch and then have a good long talk while we eat. Then I'll take my rest."

Five minutes down the trail, there's a pier that extends for ten feet into Bearpaw Lake. The blue water is held in a bowl formed by mountains that rise gray above the timberline on every side, and it reflects the sunlight in bright planes, each dazzling as the wind stirs waves on the surface. It reminds me of the sound in Seattle, of the foghorns you could hear throughout the city some early mornings. Reeds and soggy grasses weave a border at the edge of dry land, and the moving air is damp and fresh.

Father Tom wears red swimming trunks with a white stripe down the side. His body is hairy and soft and a chain with a miraculous medal circles his neck. It embarrasses me to look at him. My cutoffs, passed on to Aunt Ida for me from Foxy's mother, are too big and are cinched by an elastic stretch belt with a *Star Wars* magnetic buckle. My Holy Martyrs T-shirt has a hole under the right sleeve. In the sunlight my skin is the color of pine sap.

Sitting on the end of the dock, Father Tom sticks his white feet into the water and kicks up a spray.

"Oh, Ray," he says, laughing loudly, "it's too cold to swim. Look, I'm getting goose bumps. We'd better head back to camp."

Out about fifty feet is a wooden raft, painted yellow. Squinting past it, I can see someone canoeing on the far side of the lake.

"People are out there. I'm going in."

Without testing the water I run off the end of the dock and suddenly am surrounded by icy pinpricks, contracting my skin and blasting the tiredness. All sound is blotted out. Even the bubbles from my mouth make no noise as they rise from my lips. It's like entering a room in an empty building, like going into space. My feet sink into plants and soft mud that squeezes out between my toes as I push off. I never knew before that there are smells underwater, but there are—greens and browns. I feel totally clean.

"Rayona." Father Tom is calling at me. His voice whines. He's standing with his feet apart at the end of the pier and is upset. "You'll get a cramp. Come out."

I don't hear him.

"The water's fine," I shout and start kicking and paddling away from the shore. I'm no swimmer but I can stay afloat, and slowly I make progress. My eyes are at sea level, washed by the lake like a windshield in a rainstorm. By the time I get to the low yellow raft, I'm out of breath and chilled. I pull myself over the side and lie on the sun-warmed dry boards, panting and soaking up the heat. The silence is wide as the sky, brushed only with the sound of splashes striking the beams under the platform.

After a while I hear the crash of a dive, and watch as Father Tom sidestrokes his way out into the lake. He points his long toes with every kick, and slants his mouth to gulp air. He isn't six feet from where I rest when the noise suddenly stops and he looks at me in surprise.

"Holy Jesus," he says. "Rayona. It's too cold. I've got a cramp." Without closing his eyes his head dips into the water as he curls into a cannonball.

"Rayona," he calls when his face rolls again.

I jump, the water a freezing slap against my dry skin. He has not sunk far and lies calm and pleading when I reach his side.

"Rayona," he says a third time as I tilt his chin to the air. With my other arm grasped across his chest, I tow him toward the worn, splintery raft. His breath rasps in my ear, and he begins to sink whenever I let him go. He makes no struggle, speaks no more words. I hold on to him as I throw one of my legs, then the other, onto the flat lumber, then reaching under his arms, I drag his shoulders and chest over the edge until he cannot fall back. The rough boards scrape his skin but he won't protect himself. Finally I grab the red trunks and haul the rest of him out of the lake. He lies on his side, staring toward the shore. He starts to gasp.

I'm winded myself, but I wonder about giving him artificial respiration. I remember something about pushing on the back and pulling on the arms. I crawl to him and try to roll him onto his stomach, but at last he resists and instead turns to face me.

"You have saved me," he says, and reaching his arms around me, he pulls me close. Our chests crowd together and I feel the pound of his heart as the medal he wears digs into me. He's colder than the lake, so frozen that it burns where our skin touches.

"We are alone," he says, and moves to line the length of his body against me. We are the same size, from toe to head. He presses, presses, presses, and the air leaves my lungs. I want to sleep, to drown, to bore deep within the boards of the raft.

Father Tom has ducked his head, has closed his eyes tight. His hips jerk against me.

In my dream I move with him, pin him to me with my strong arms, search for his face with my mouth.

His body freezes. It turns to stone. I release my hold and we fall apart. I breathe.

"What are you doing?" Father Tom whispers.

"I don't know," I say. "I was afraid. I don't swim that good."

He sits, swivels away from me.

I roll onto my back. It's still the same day and the sky is blue.

"I'd say you swim pretty well," he says.

The skin on his stomach is red and chafed from the boards. He hugs his knees to his chest. He shakes his head, as if he has water in his ears. He's busy thinking.

"Rayona, we have experienced an occasion of sin." He doesn't look at me as he speaks. "What would your parents think? I could be your father. I have taken vows."

I hear the blame in his voice and I tense to defend myself. It occurs to me to say my parents wouldn't be surprised, that nothing happened, that he was the one that started it.

"I made up all that about him being a pilot. He's a mailman."

Father Tom makes a sound like a crow. I can't tell if he is laughing or crying or clearing his throat of the last drops of swallowed lake.

"We must go back to the reservation," he says finally. "We should never have come."

"What about the jamboree?" I ask Father Tom, but he slides off the raft and into the water. This time he has no trouble swimming. In fact, he is already half dressed, pulling his black pants over his wet swimming suit, by the time I reach the pier. What little hair he has, above his ears and on the back of his head, stands out like some sort of halo from where the towel has rubbed it.

"Rayona," he says, "I should never have gone in when I was so tired. I had no rest. You understand that? When we get back, we should forget this trip ever happened. It was a bad idea, something I should have foreseen. You need friends your own age. Some people might misunderstand if they see us together all the time."

He's cracking his knuckles again. The sound they make is as loud and hollow as a woodpecker hammering against a dead tree.

"I'm not going back. I'm going to Seattle."

"Oh yes, Seattle. I'm sure you have somewhere to live in the city?"

"There are lots of places. I could look up my dad."

"That might be just the thing for you to do." He acts as if this is funny. He nods his head, making the halo wave like October grass in the wind.

I turn away from him and pull my too-big pants over my too-big wet cutoffs. I'm afraid of him, the way he's behaving.

"Rayona? Are you serious?"

"Yes," I say, trying to keep my voice tough.

"Do you have any money?"

I don't.

"Well, if you're truly set on going, maybe I can lend you some cash for the ticket and for cab fare from the train. To tide you over."

I don't answer him.

"Are you positive that this is what you want?"

He's getting interested in the idea of my departure. He skips flat rocks on the lake while I finish dressing.

"You know," Father Tom says, "it doesn't really make a lot of sense for you to come all the way back to the reservation with me if you're going to Seattle. It's the wrong direction. I noticed there's a depot right at the park entrance."

There's no stopping him now.

"A ticket would be cheaper from here. I can put you on the train and with what you save you can take your dad out to dinner. I can retrieve anything you need from your aunt's and send it on to you."

Yesterday he didn't believe in this Dad. Now he's buying him a meal.

"I should tell Aunt Ida." I should tell Mom too, I think.

But he's ready for that.

"I'll make a special trip there the minute I return and explain the whole thing to her. Don't worry. I'll make sure she's all right."

I try to imagine him talking to Aunt Ida. I feel bad that she should find out from him, but I can't admit it. Whatever she thinks about my leaving, he'll never know.

I can't think of another reason that will get me back, so I walk the trail to the campsite with my head buzzing. We collect our things and load them in the truck without exchanging another word.

In the next town, Father Tom calls the Great Northern ticket office to find out about the train. They report it comes through at 10:17 tonight. Father Tom buys me a hamburger and a *Sports Illustrated* to read, and keeps going on about how interesting Seattle must be—a lot like Milwaukee, which is one of his favorite places—and what a bright young lady like me can do there.

"And you won't feel so alone, so out of place," he says, smiling that stupid grin of his. "There'll be others in a community of that size who share your dual heritage."

The hours of that endless afternoon pass, and at last we sit in the cab of the truck, waiting by the crossing for the engine's beam to slice into the night. When it does, Father Tom is supposed to blink the truck headlamps three times and the train will stop to let me board. We have fallen quiet, with nothing more to say to each other.

I feel the rumble from the earth before I see the light. First the tires, then the worn springs of the truck begin to quiver and shake.

Father Tom blinks his brights once, twice, three times and the sound starts to cut down. The night beyond the tracks' illumination is very dark.

"Rayona, I want you to have this."

He pulls something over his head. I think it's the holy medal that cut into my chest at the lake and I reach to take it, but it's only the beaded medallion he wears on the reservation, big and gaudy. Tourist bait.

"Wear this. Then people will know you're an Indian." He gets out of the cab at the same time I do, as the train continues to slow, and stuffs some dollar bills into my jeans pocket. Through the cloth I feel his fingers.

"Don't worry about repayment. I know we'll meet again."

He grabs me to him, quick and hard, then pushes me away just as fast.

"I'm going to leave you now, Rayona. I'm bad at good-byes. You'll be in my prayers."

He climbs into the truck and backs it to the black tree line before hitting the lights. Then he revs the engine and turns onto the highway, heading east.

He doesn't look at me, so he doesn't see me wave the train on, or hear the engineer yell a fast-moving curse at goddamn Indians playing tricks. He doesn't see me toss his medallion onto the track to be ground into plastic dust.

When the earth has stopped trembling, when the sounds of wind and frogs and crickets have returned, I stand alone in the cold night. Clouds block the sky and all directions are the same. I can smell the lake. I've never felt further from sleep.

I search and cue memories of Dad that would allow me to believe he'd be glad if I appeared out of the blue, but there aren't enough. I try recalling what Mom says when she's sentimental and lonesome: how he was the best one, the only one, because he left her me. How I'm her sterling silver lining, the one who'll never leave her like he did.

Like she did me.

I hunch into a pocket of gravel between two ties and lean back against the track, still warm from the train's passing. I settle in, roll my head so I can see through the tree limbs as the clouds slide across the sky. I'm in a tight spot but it could be worse. I have the priest's money and the whole night to think before morning comes. I'm happy without reason.

ACKNOWLEDGMENTS

I would like to thank the authors included for their permission to reprint, my colleagues at Oklahoma Geary Hobson and Maurice Kenny for their support and advice, and most of all my indefatigable research assistant, Maureen Bannon, who did all the dreary jobs cheerfully.

The following selections are used by the kind permission of the publishers listed here.

Library of Congress Cataloging-
in-Publication Data
The Lightning within: an
anthology of contemporary
American Indian fiction/
edited and with an introduction
by Alan R. Velie.
p.   cm.
ISBN 0-8032-4659-5
(cl: alk. paper)
1. American fiction—Indian
authors.   2. Indians of
North America—Fiction.
3. American fiction—20th century.
I. Velie, Alan R., 1937–   .
PS508.I5L54   1991
813'.54080897—dc20
90-12658   CIP